IT STARTED IN *Paradise*

NICKI NIGHT

HARLEQUIN® KIMANI™ ROMANCE

London Borough of Hackney	
91300001054765	
Askews & Holts	
AF ROM	£6.50
	5607466

Recycling programs for this product may not exist in your area.

ISBN-13: 978-0-373-86506-2

It Started in Paradise

Printed in U.S.A.

This book is dedicated to my hero, Les Flagler.
I love the way you love me, Sunshine.

Acknowledgments

As always, I begin by thanking my Lord and Savior,
Jesus Christ. Without him, there wouldn't be any books,
readers, contracts, writing…anything.
I'm so grateful for this journey.

I offer up a special shout-out to my squad at
Harlequin Kimani, Glenda Howard and Keyla Hernandez,
for all you do. To Sara Camilli, agent extraordinaire,
thanks for great conversation, guidance
and for always having my back.

Thank you to my family,
who doesn't mind sharing me with my dreams.
I appreciate you Les, Lil Les, Milan (Hollywood) and
Laila (Suga Mama). To the Daniels clan and my gals,
thank you for your continued support.

To my sisters and brothers in the craft,
I adore and respect you. Let's do this!

My mentors, Beverly Jenkins and Beverly Jackson,
I appreciate that you don't mind pouring into me.
You are amazing women.

To my street team, I don't know what I'd do without you.
Thanks for all you do.

Reviewers, bloggers, readers…you completely ROCK!
That's it and that's all.

Nicki Night is an edgy hopeless romantic who enjoys creating stories of love and new possibilities. Nicki has a penchant for adventure and is currently working on penning her next romantic escapade. Nicki resides in the city dreams are made of, but occasionally travels to her treasured seaside hideaway to write in seclusion. She enjoys hearing from readers and can be contacted on Facebook, through her website at nickinight.com, or via email at nickinightwrites@gmail.com.

Books by Nicki Night

Harlequin Kimani Romance

Her Chance at Love
His Love Lesson
Riding into Love
It Started in Paradise

Visit the Author Profile page
at Harlequin.com for more titles.

Chapter 1

"I saw you looking at him," Jewel Chandler teased her older sister, sipped her cocktail and then lay back on her lounge chair.

Chloe Chandler choked back a laugh. "I wasn't looking at anyone." Turning her head in the other direction, she shielded her eyes from the glaring sun. She'd seen him all right. All six feet four inches of his muscular frame draped in skin so rich and smooth, it could have been dripping from a fondue pot.

"Humph! Whatever you say, Sissy." Jewel waved her off. "There's never been anything wrong with looking. It's the touching that gets people in trouble! But who am I to tell you to play by anybody's rules?"

"Exactly. Now hush!" Chloe laughed. As the oldest, she'd always been careful to set a good example. Not that it helped at all. All three of her younger siblings were rebels in their own rights.

Donovan Rivers jumped into the hotel's Olympic-size pool, sliced through the water as smoothly as a knife cutting ice cream and popped up on the opposite side. The water cascading down his taut back made Chloe hiss.

Jewel sat up, lifted her wide-brimmed hat meant to block the sun and tilted her sunglasses downward. "You're a liar if you tell me you didn't see that gorgeousness rise from that water like a Greek god." Jewel sat back and chuckled.

Chloe couldn't help but laugh with her. "No one wants Donovan."

"And there's another lie."

"Jewel!"

Jewel twisted her lips at Chloe. "Plenty of women want him. I happen to know a few of them rather well and so do you. Humph! A woman would be crazy not to want a man like him or his brother."

"You know our mother would have an emotional breakdown if one of us were to mess around with one of those Rivers boys." Chloe lay back on her lounger, closed her eyes and crossed her feet.

"And that is just what makes it so much fun. Forbidden fruit is always the sweetest!" Jewel snickered.

Chloe sat up. "What?"

She laughed full out this time.

Chloe's eyes widened and her mouth fell open. "Have you messed around with one of those Rivers men?" Chloe wouldn't put it past her sister.

"Sure did, and it was good and so much fun!"

"And you never told me?" Still seated, Chloe parked her hands on her hips.

"Nope!" Jewel pursed her lips.

Offended, Chloe gasped. There were never any secrets among the sisters. "When?"

"Last summer, and I never said anything because you would have told me not to do it." Jewel swung her legs over the deck chair and faced Chloe. "I wanted to do it. I did it and I liked it—a lot!" She squealed. "It only lasted a few delicious weeks but then we moved on. It was more like…" Jewel thought for a moment "…an extended fling, but it certainly was fun while it lasted."

Chloe squeezed her eyes shut and shook her head. "I can't believe you! Was it Donovan?"

"No. It was Dayton." Jewel closed her eyes and moaned as if she'd eaten a decadent bite of dessert.

Chloe giggled, despite feeling snubbed. The talk about the forbidden rendezvous made her giddy. Her sisters lived much riskier lives than she ever had. One day she'd take a page from their book. "I still can't believe you hid that juicy little tidbit from me." Chloe tossed her towel at Jewel. She blocked it.

"I'm sorry." Jewel pouted. "Do you forgive me?"

"Of course I do, but don't ever leave me out of the loop again."

"Good. I won't. I promise," Jewel said before standing. "You need to get yourself a piece of forbidden action someday, too. You won't believe how delightful it can be." Jewel slid her arms through her sheer white cover-up. "Perhaps Donovan could be the perfect candidate."

"Oh no!" Chloe wagged her finger. "I don't think so."

Jewel flashed a sly smile. "Don't worry. I wouldn't tell anyone."

Chloe rolled her eyes toward the sky. "I'm not indulging in this foolishness." She stood too, grabbed her cell phone and the magazine she'd intended to read at the poolside but never opened. "Let's go get ready for our dinner meeting."

"I'm going to get you to loosen up one of these days, Sissy. You can't be all work and no play all the time."

"I have plenty of fun." Chloe headed toward the hotel but stopped when she sensed that Jewel wasn't walking with her.

She looked back to find Jewel with her hand propped on her hip, lips twisted and head tilted. She obviously didn't agree with Chloe.

"Come on, silly!" Chloe waved her along. "This pavement is scorching." She dropped her flip-flops on the ground and stuck her feet in them.

Jewel fell into stride next to Chloe. "I bet you've never had a one-night stand."

Chloe's mouth dropped, then closed quickly. She looked around to make sure no one else at the resort heard Jewel's comment. "No, I haven't!" She stood erect but then leaned closer to Jewel. "Have you?" she whispered.

Jewel's response was a loud cackle. The laugh lasted several moments. When Jewel was able to catch her breath and regain her composure, she looked at Chloe pitifully, shaking her head. Chloe crossed her arms over her chest and glared back at Jewel.

"Sissy. You've got to learn to live a little."

"I don't need to have sex with strangers in order to *live a little*," Chloe mocked and then turned abruptly, heading for the door.

"Don't be mad. I just want you to have some adventure." Jewel trotted after Chloe. "A one-night stand isn't necessarily with a stranger. Mine wasn't."

Jewel's words softened Chloe's resolve. "I'll show you I'm capable of being adventurous after we handle business at this dinner tonight."

"I'm going to hold you to that."

Chloe discreetly looked back toward the pool to see if Donovan was still around.

"I saw that!" Jewel said without losing her stride.

"You saw what?" Chloe feigned innocence.

"You've never been a good liar." Jewel's shoulders shook as she chuckled. "He left the pool about five minutes ago."

Chloe decided not to try to deny the fact that she wanted to get one last glimpse at Donovan's sculpted body. Jewel was right. Looking had never hurt anyone. Touching Donovan was something else altogether.

Chloe had no time for men anyway. Her job kept her busy. Loving what she did made it easy to work all day long and sometimes well into the night. Eager to impress her boss, who was also her mother, she didn't mind putting in the extra hours.

Thinking about work brought to mind her reason for visiting Puerto Rico. As scenic as the views were and as pleasing as it was to gaze at Donovan's perfect body from a distance, she was there for business, not pleasure.

Chloe hadn't been looking for Donovan Rivers, but as he was the heir to La Belle Riviere, a coveted venue for lavish events along Long Island's Gold Coast, she wasn't surprised to see him at the International Food and Beverage Convention. The little bit of sun she and Jewel had just soaked up was probably all they would have time for since their schedules were packed for the rest of their stay. The next few days were filled with sessions, business meetings and then the revered awards dinner.

Chloe's goal was to return home to New York with strategies for making their restaurant on the pier a more sought-after venue for high-profile events. Jewel's goal was to find out the latest technology in packaging for their family's consumer goods dynasty, Chandler Food Corp. Jewel was also looking into the latest in appliances for the renovation that their father planned for their company's kitchen.

Chloe couldn't focus on Donovan in any serious manner anyway. Despite the close proximity in which their families lived, both literally and figuratively, getting involved with Donovan would be highly problematic due to the level of hostility that existed between their families—specifically their mothers.

Elnora, or El as most called her, could hardly stomach the sight of Donovan's mother, the refined and oh-so-esteemed Joliet Rivers. Chloe and her sisters had never been told of the history behind their situation but they did know not to socialize with the Rivers children even now as adults.

Donovan was the oldest of his siblings and had always been extremely attractive. Chloe had her fill admiring him from a distance.

Jewel and Chloe showered and were outfitted in dresses that were comfortable but polished enough for conducting business. Their dinner meeting would be with a potential supplier of industrial appliances who wanted to show Jewel his state-of-the-art equipment. After that, they were scheduled to have drinks with a consultant who was interested in helping their family take Chandlers, their restaurant on the marina where Chloe served as the director of events, to the next level.

Jewel pushed the call button for the elevator and the doors opened right up. They stepped in chatting about their evening. As the elevator doors began to close, a strong hand reached in and waved. The doors slid back open.

Donovan's statuesque frame entered as if he were floating across the red carpet at an awards show. His well-fitting gray suit highlighted his broad shoulders and slim waist and the pleasant scent of his cologne made the small space mannishly aromatic.

"How are you, Jewel?" He nodded. "Chloe." He nodded again, winked and his lush lips slid into an easy smile as he swept Chloe with his gaze from head to toe.

Chloe's stomach tightened.

"I'm well, Donovan, and you?" Jewel was cheerful. Too cheerful, Chloe thought.

"Doing well," he said, still facing Chloe's direction.

Jewel turned to Chloe also. She still hadn't responded.

"Donovan." She nodded in a refined manner, just as her mother would have.

Jewel and Donovan engaged in small talk for the short ride. To Chloe, the air in the elevator seemed to have thinned. She cleared her throat, painted on a regal smile and held her head high until the doors opened on the lobby level.

Donovan stepped out first. With his back against the door, he held his hand out. "After you."

"Thank you," the women said in unison.

"My pleasure," Donovan said with a sexy glance directed at Chloe.

"We should get together for drinks while we're out here," Jewel said.

"We should." Donovan stepped aside to keep from blocking the elevator. "What are you doing later tonight?"

"We don't have anything planned after our meetings," Jewel said.

Chloe just smiled.

"Me neither." Donovan reached inside his suit jacket and retrieved his cell phone. "Take my number. Let's confer when we're done. I know a great place."

"Cool!" Jewel took out her phone and tapped in his number.

"Chloe, what's your number?" Donovan's voice warmed her ears.

Chloe swallowed and gave it to him.

"Good! I'll see you ladies later." Donovan's light touch to Chloe's shoulder sent slight tremors down her back.

"Damn, that man is gorgeous," Jewel said as he walked away.

Chloe winced, hoping Donovan hadn't heard her. "Come on. We have people waiting for us," Chloe said, dismissing Jewel's acknowledgment of the obvious.

"Maybe he could be your first one-night stand," Jewel teased.

Chloe stopped walking and swatted Jewel's arm. "You're unbelievable." She laughed. "That's not going to happen." She continued walking.

"Never say never!" Jewel sang.

Chloe kept her mouth shut but allowed the possibilities to roll around in her mind even though she couldn't see it happening in real life.

Chapter 2

Donovan peered across the dim, busy restaurant and spotted his friend. Merengue blared through speakers tucked into the ceiling. The volume elevated to a level that made it difficult for him to hear his own thoughts. Donovan snaked through tables sideways and then weaved through a crowd of dancers yelping and winding their hips to the rhythm pulsating through the restaurant like a collective heartbeat.

"You made it!" Keenan tapped the stool next to him. "I saved you a seat." The two shook hands.

"Great to see you! I think someone touched my behind on the way over here." Donovan looked back toward the dance floor. A woman in a white ruffled blouse and red flowing skirt winked as she three-stepped from one side to the other. "Yeah, I'm pretty sure that happened."

"There's a good chance that it did in here." Keenan laughed. "How's the conference going?"

"I haven't done much yet." Donovan lifted his hand to signal the waiter. "My flight got in early. After settling in, I did a little sightseeing and spent the rest of the afternoon at the pool. I tried to take advantage of what little downtime I have. How's business coming along?"

"The deal looks like it's going to happen." Keenan took a sip of amber liquid after swirling it in his glass.

"That's great!" The waiter arrived and Donovan ordered his drink in Spanish. "I'm glad we were able to get together for a drink before you left."

"I know. We're like two vessels crossing. You come the day before I leave." Keenan sat back and gave Donovan a pensive look. "The offer still stands."

Donovan sighed. "I appreciate it but my plate is full."

"I know the resort would do well with you heading up the events department. It's a great venue for weddings and conferences. I'd like to see you take on a larger role than just being an investor on this project. And the money." Keenan whistled. "We're going to make a ton. The seller got into some legal trouble and he's offloading his properties for ridiculously low prices."

"You make an attractive offer, but to be effective I'd have to stay here for extended periods of time. Right now my father's relying on me to expand our business back home. We're contemplating renovations, hiring consultants, ramping up our PR efforts and all kinds of stuff. I almost didn't make it here for this conference, but I worked it out and was able to schedule a few important meetings." Donovan looked down the bar for the bartender. "You just make sure I have a special suite for when I visit Puerto Rico. Let the staff know they have to treat me well. Ha!"

"That will certainly be taken care of."

The bartender finally arrived, set Donovan's drink in front of him and napkin beside it. He waited for Donovan's nod of approval before leaving. "How's the family?" he asked Keenan.

"Everyone is great. My parents are moving to Miami. My dad said he's done with New York winters. Jackson opened a private investigation company and he's doing extremely well. He didn't expect all the disgruntled spouses but they pay well." Keenan's laugh settled into a wide smile. "I'm getting married."

"Wow!" Donovan sat back and patted Keenan's shoulder.

"Congratulations, man! I haven't seen Adriana since graduation. Is she still in banking?"

"She runs a brokerage firm now. Miami has been good to her." Keenan placed his empty glass on the bar top. The waiter held his finger up, questioning if Keenan wanted another. Keenan held his hand up in return, letting the bartender know he was done. "Graduation," he said reminiscently. "So much has changed since then."

"Yeah." Fond memories of days in their Ivy League graduate program flashed across Donovan's mind. "All good things."

After catching up, they went back to talking business. Keenan shared the renovation plans and reviewed the finances for the resort his company was in the process of purchasing. Even though Donovan's only role was that of an investor, Keenan gave him a thorough update, promising to keep him informed through the entire process.

Donovan felt confident about the money he'd invested in the endeavor and looked forward to gaining a robust return. If this went well, there were resorts in other areas of the island they wanted to explore. After that, they'd see about getting property in other tropical cities as well.

When business had been handled, Keenan stood and Donovan followed his lead.

"Great seeing you, man," Donovan said. They hugged.

"I wish I could hang around longer but I need to head back to the other side of the island since I'm on the first flight out in the morning. Next time we need to coordinate our travel better so we can really hang out. I don't get to see anyone since I moved to Miami."

"Tell Adriana I said hello and good luck with the wedding."

"You're going to come down for it, aren't you?" Keenan asked.

"I wouldn't miss it."

Donovan and Keenan walked out together. Both had drivers waiting to take them back to their respective hotels, where Donovan headed straight to the lobby bar in search of Chloe and Jewel. He checked his watch and then texted the ladies.

Jewel responded first, letting him know that they were still in their meeting and should be done soon. They agreed to meet up in an hour. That gave Donovan enough time to freshen up and change into casual clothing.

Donovan walked through the lobby, stepping in time with the rhythm of the music floating from the lobby bar. The day had been productive and he felt good about that. Now it was time to relax and enjoy the evening essence of beautiful Puerto Rico and he looked forward to doing that with the Chandler sisters—especially Chloe.

Since they were children, he'd always been aware of her. Donovan chuckled. What would his mother think? She would certainly be upset, but as much as he loved his mother, Donovan was his own man. Besides, tonight would be nothing more than an opportunity to unwind with friends—friends that just happen to be quite beautiful despite their familial history.

In the hotel suite, Donovan got dressed and slipped into a pair of slacks and a button-down shirt before squirting on a few splashes of cologne. This time, he opted for the tiki bar outside of the hotel.

Salsa mixed with the sounds of the waves offered audible splendor. A cool breeze caressed his arms. Donovan smiled in response. Finding a table that provided the best view of the moonlit ocean, he sat facing the water as he waited for his server. A young man with a long ponytail, untamed facial hair and a floral shirt approached shortly after.

"I'll take your best scotch," Donovan said.

"Sure." The waiter scribbled Donovan's order on a pad.

"Wait. No." He thought better of his decision to indulge in his signature selection. He was in the tropics. Why not order accordingly? "What do you recommend?"

"Rum, of course!" His accent made his words sound like music. "I'll bring something you'll like. Trust me?"

"I'll go for it." Donovan nodded in agreement.

"Be right back."

As the waiter walked off, Donovan sat back in his chair, allowing the tropical breeze to soothe him. His mind drifted. What was it going to be like when Jewel and Chloe joined him later?

Chapter 3

"Great meetings. I'm really excited about the renovation now. I can't wait to get back and share this information with Mom," Chloe said to Jewel as she headed toward her room. She stepped out of her dress and laid it on the bed.

A few minutes later, Jewel joined Chloe in her room. "Technology is an amazing thing. We'll be able to produce more pies using the same amount of space. We'll never have a problem meeting demand now—especially during the holidays." Posing in the mirror, Jewel checked out the flowing jumpsuit she'd just put on.

"How's this?" Chloe presented herself to Jewel, twirling in the floral strapless sundress she'd selected for the evening.

"Oh! Very pretty." Jewel offered a wide smile. "Donovan's going to love that," she teased.

"I'm not thinking about Donovan." Chloe waved her off and slipped her feet into a pair of beaded flip-flops.

"You should be. It's been months since you've dated—about a year, actually."

"And I'm fine with that. Who's counting anyway?" Chloe shrugged.

"Me! And so should you. It's time to get back in the game." Jewel put her hand on the doorknob. "Ready?"

"Yeah." Chloe walked through the open door. "Truthfully, Jewel, I've been so into work I've hardly thought about it. I'm thrilled about taking the restaurant to another level. Chandlers can really become the sought-after venue for events once we start working with this consultant. It's time to elevate our brand. When you love what you do, it's easy to be caught up. After my breakup with Alan, the days and months have just rolled right on by."

"Mom loved that guy for some reason."

"I know. She just knew that he was going to be her son-in-law. At first, I thought that he would be the one, too. He seemed refined, debonair and worldly. He relished living up to the image of what we represented—two successful people with all the appropriate fixings and a glamorous lifestyle. I wanted genuine romance. I didn't care what we looked like. Warm hugs, kisses, cozy movie nights and long walks are the things that I craved. He wanted to be seen at every major function. We just couldn't seem to find our middle ground. I'd end up at home while he attended his high-profile parties. Eventually, we just grew apart. As much as it hurt, we both knew it was best to end the relationship. Mom will never get it."

They had arrived at the elevator. Jewel pressed the call button and sighed. "I completely understand but I still think it's time that you get out. I know it's easy to get so involved in what you're doing that you forget to have a life and I don't want to see that happen to you any longer."

"You're right. I can't remember the last time I had dinner with someone and it wasn't about business."

The elevator doors opened and the two of them stepped on.

"No better time to start than the present. Let's go have some fun, girl. Woo!" Jewel raised a fist in the air.

Chloe shook her head at Jewel's loud hoot, but laughed. She had to agree, it was time to begin carving a little extra-curricular fun into her life. Loving what she did for a living shouldn't prevent her from enjoying a fuller existence.

Perhaps she'd start with a girls' night out with her sisters and friends when she got back to New York.

A bustling lobby greeted them when the elevator doors opened. A festive vibe had taken over now that the evening had given way to the night. Music, laughter and jovial conversations in various languages blended like a symphony. Shorts, floral shirts and casual dresses replaced the business attire from earlier in the day.

Chloe and Jewel snaked through the crowd toward the outdoor bar that Donovan had directed them to via text. Chloe's stomach clenched when she spotted Donovan's handsome profile outlined by the glow of the moon. He was seated with his head resting against the back of the chair. He was gorgeous from every angle.

Chloe looked forward to hanging out with him. Though they'd operated within the same social circles for many years, they'd never spent much time together. Tonight, she'd get to know him a little better.

Donovan stood as they approached. Kissing both their cheeks, his lips lingered against Chloe's for just a moment longer. His hand gently pressed against her lower back, causing shivers inside her core. She stepped back and smiled graciously and then turned toward the calming sound of the ocean waves. She closed her eyes and breathed deeply to compose herself rather than to delight in the ambiance.

"Have a seat." Donovan pulled out a chair for both. The low timbre of his voice caused her core to react once again.

"Thanks." She sat first and then Jewel.

"It's beautiful out here," Jewel acknowledged.

"There's something mysterious about the sea at night. It's frightening, yet intriguing," Chloe said. When she looked up, Donovan was staring at her. She held his gaze for a moment and cleared her throat. "I've always wondered what it must be like to be out there in all that darkness."

"It's pretty cool," Donovan said.

"Is it?" Jewel asked. "How so?"

"It's peaceful. I took one of those midnight cruises before. We should see if they do those here at this hotel."

"Oh. Let's check into that. Sounds like fun." Jewel turned to Chloe. "Doesn't it?"

"It does." Chloe sat back, allowing the breeze to relax her. It was almost as satisfying as Donovan's presence.

Donovan waved the waiter over. "What are you ladies having?"

"I had this great drink by the pool earlier. It was fruity with rum in it," Jewel said.

"I could use a nice glass of wine," Chloe added.

As the waiter approached, Donovan nodded toward the women. "May I?" he asked, requesting their permission to order for them.

Chloe and Jewel looked at each other. Agreeing with raised brows, Chloe then turned to Donovan and said, "Sure."

Donovan ordered wine for Chloe and a rum cocktail for Jewel.

"What are they doing over there?" Chloe leaned forward, squinting at a few of the bar's staff members setting up speakers and a large projection screen against the backdrop of the dark ocean.

Donovan and Jewel turned toward Chloe's line of sight.

"Are they showing a movie tonight?" Jewel inquired.

Donovan shrugged. "Perhaps."

"How cool!" Chloe added. The idea of watching a movie under the velvet star-spangled sky charmed her. "How were your meetings today?" she asked Donovan.

"Pretty good." Donovan told them about his day and the hotel his friend was renovating. The waiter returned with their drinks. They nodded their approval, which Donovan acknowledged with a confident smile.

"That sounds amazing! Let us know if he does a grand opening. We could come down to celebrate with you," Jewel said.

"That would be great. I'll make sure you have the best accommodations." His comment was for both women, but his eyes were on Chloe.

If she wasn't mistaken, there was more meaning behind his words that were spoken. His slightly narrowed gaze and the sultry smile that spread across his sexy lips gave her that indication.

Chloe felt warmth settle around her like a soft blanket. She matched his gaze for a moment before turning and looking out over the water.

"Just make sure we're on the opposite side of the hotel from your mother," she said and the three of them laughed.

"You're right about that," Donovan admitted. "If she knew we were here having a good time together, she'd probably faint."

"I know," Jewel added, releasing a belly laugh. "What's up with them?"

Donovan shook his head. "I don't know. My mother would never tell us."

"Neither would ours," Chloe said.

"It's so crazy to me," Jewel said.

"Me, too," Chloe agreed. "Whatever it is, it has been going on for a long time."

"That's one thing I do know." Donovan took another a sip of his rum and pointed toward the setup the bar staff was working on. "Looks like they're setting up for kara-oke."

"Really?" Chloe got excited.

"Chloe. You should sing," Jewel said, craning her neck

toward the screen. "Donovan, you've got to hear her. She has an amazing voice."

Donovan looked at Chloe and raised a brow. "Is that so?"

Chloe waved her hand dismissively and cast her eyes upward. "I don't sing much. I haven't done it in years."

"She's totally being modest." Jewel grabbed Chloe's hand and pulled her up. "Come on, let's go pick a song. I'll be your backup!" she hooted.

"Jewel!" Chloe pleaded but was ignored as Jewel dragged her over to the table that had been set up for people to sign up.

"I can't sing here," Chloe said, feeling nervous.

"Of course you can. Didn't you say you wanted to start having more fun?"

Chloe groaned. "Let me look over the list." Jewel squealed and Chloe squinted at her. "I didn't say I was going to sing. I'm just checking this list out."

Jewel handed her the clipboard containing the songs and peered at it over Chloe's shoulder. "Oh. Do this one." Jewel pointed to *Natural Woman.*

Chloe thought about it for a moment. She loved singing that song but the idea of doing so in front of Donovan would make her feel exposed. She already felt overtly aware of her senses in his presence.

People used to love listening to her jazzy voice. She'd won several talent competitions but she hadn't sung in front of anyone besides her sisters since her mother chided her years ago for wasting time at an audition for a performing arts school. According to El, Chloe was going to be a successful businesswoman and the notion of her daughter attending school to sing was a ridiculous misuse of her time and energy. Her days of public crooning had ended then. She was disappointed but wouldn't disobey her mother.

"I don't know, Jewel." She frowned. "I haven't sung in a long time."

"It's just for fun." Jewel pouted. "Please…for me. I love hearing you sing. Come on, Chloe."

"What are you going to sing?"

Chloe spun around at the sound of Donovan's voice. She hadn't realized he'd come over to where they were.

"I'm still trying to convince her," Jewel said.

"I'll sing if you sing first." Chloe raised a brow at Donovan.

"If you don't mind the torture. I couldn't hold a note if it was duct-taped to my chest but it's all in good fun, right?"

"Exactly! All in good fun," Jewel endorsed Donovan.

Chloe exhaled. "You first." She pointed to Donovan.

"Whatever. Let me see what's on this list." Donovan took the clipboard from Jewel. His eyes scanned the paper and within seconds he tapped his finger on the selection sheet. "I'll do this one." Donovan selected a popular rap song from the late nineties.

Chloe and Jewel bent over laughing. "I can't wait to see this," Chloe said.

Each of them signed up for a song and headed back to their table.

"This is going to be epic!" Jewel cracked up.

They ordered more drinks while the people before them took to the karaoke microphone. Enjoying themselves immensely, they sang along with a group of men who hilariously performed the YMCA song. An obviously intoxicated woman with a nasally sounding voice sang an out-of-tune rendition of *Love Shack*. By the time she hit the last note, she and the entire audience were doubled over laughing. Being a great sport, she finished with an impressive bow as if she'd just brought down the house with a stellar performance.

It was Donovan's turn. He took to the microphone with

confidence. The music started and he captured Chloe's gaze and smiled. She blushed, tickled by the way his smile affected her.

"Go, Donovan!" Jewel cheered him on.

Donovan pointed at Jewel and winked.

The words came up and Donovan missed the first line. He jumped in, tripping over the words in the second line until he caught up. He was off tune but clearly didn't care. He swayed to the music and poorly belted out the words until he was breathless.

The crowd cheered him on. Jewel and Chloe both had tears streaming down their faces as they laughed and sang along. Donovan waved his hands instructing the crowd to join him. By the time he finished, everyone was waving and singing. Donovan stepped off the stage as confidently as he had stepped on.

"Your turn," he said to Chloe when he got back to where they were seated.

"You did a fine job," Jewel teased. They all laughed.

If Donovan could make a complete fool of himself in front of all those people, why should Chloe feel nervous? She had to admit she was having a great time.

The crowd settled down and the announcer called Chloe's name. Her stomach fluttered but she stood and made her way over to the stage. She took the microphone and looked out over the crowd. Closing her eyes, she swallowed and took a deep breath. When she opened her eyes, she noticed her hand trembling. She held the microphone with both hands to ease the shaking. The music started. Anticipating her performance, the crowd quieted. She felt exposed and tried to remember that she was there to have fun.

"You got this, Chloe!" Jewel yelled, which generated other random supportive shouts from the crowd.

"You can do it, girl!" one woman yelled.

"Have fun with it," another said.

"Chloe!" Donovan's deep voice reached her. When she looked over he was clapping, encouraging her in the distance.

Chloe closed her eyes and started singing. She didn't need the words. Her exquisite voice floated out over the audience. Whistles, applause and whoops erupted from the crowd.

"Sing, honey!" someone else shouted.

Suddenly, the crowd no longer existed to Chloe. The joy of singing returned, rushing over her like the waves crashing into the shore.

Chloe removed one hand from the microphone and got so into the song that when she finished, she felt like she had blacked out. Cheers exploded from the audience, jolting her back to time and space. She opened her eyes and people were jumping up and down and whistling high-pitched shrieks through fingers. The standing ovation lasted until she'd made it all the way back to her seat where she found Jewel in tears and Donovan's mouth agape.

Jewel wrapped her arms around her sister. "Oh my goodness! Chloe, that was absolutely beautiful!"

When Jewel finally pulled back, Chloe's eyes met Donovan's. This time she saw something different staring back at her. It was more than a flirtatious gesture. It was something stronger and magnetic that pulled her to him.

"That was amazing," Donovan said, pinning her with his gaze.

"Thank you." Chloe lowered her eyes, unable to withstand the intensity of his stare any longer.

In that moment, something new kindled between them. Emotions shifted. Chloe wondered if Donovan felt it, too.

Chapter 4

The sound of Chloe's beautiful voice reached down deep inside Donovan and triggered something. When she returned from the stage in that flowing sundress, he couldn't take his eyes off her. Curiosities emerged and suddenly he wanted to find out more about her. Of course he'd known all about her family and where she'd grown up, but now he wanted to know more intimate things about her. What made her smile?

They continued to hang out for a while longer, listening to those bold enough to take to the microphone. Some were great, most were intoxicated and fumbled over the words to the songs they sang. Many were hilariously horrible, causing laughter to erupt, filling the beach with inebriated elation.

Despite the fact that Donovan had an early start to look forward to the next morning, he stayed by the bar talking to Chloe and Jewel well into the night. Jewel excused herself to use the restroom, leaving him alone with Chloe. At first, she squirmed under the scrutiny of his gaze. He enjoyed the fact that he affected her in some way. Perhaps she was curious about him as well.

Chloe closed her eyes and appeared to enjoy the breeze that washed over her. Donovan took that moment to admire how the moon cast soft light across her supple skin. Her shoulder-length hair danced gracefully with the wind. He found himself wanting to trace the outline of her nose and lips with his fingertips and run his fingers through her hair. She opened her eyes and he smiled.

"You never told me you could sing like that." Donovan started conversation to shift his focus. He could have stared at her until the sun returned, but he knew that would have made her uncomfortable.

She chuckled. "When would I have had the opportunity to tell you?"

"You've got a point." Donovan emptied the last of his drink. "You know what's funny?"

"What?" Chloe asked, finally turning to fully face him.

Chloe blinked and Donovan could have sworn time slackened to slow motion. She fixed her doe eyes directly on him. His body reacted with a spasm in his groin.

"We've known each other since we were kids, attended the same schools and lived within the same social circles for years and there's still a lot I don't know about you."

"You're right," Chloe acknowledged.

"We should do something about that." His desire flew past his lips before he had a chance to filter the thought.

Chloe cleared her throat.

"How about dinner tomorrow night?" *Why waste time*, Donovan thought. He wanted to learn more about Chloe Chandler and he had no intentions of toying with his interest. "I know a beautiful place on the other side of the island."

"That should be fine." Chloe looked at her watch and then looked toward the resort's entrance. "Let me check with Jewel and make sure—"

"Just you and I," Donovan interjected.

"Oh..." Chloe's surprise and coyness made him smile once again.

"I'm sure Jewel wouldn't mind but do check with her to make sure. I wouldn't want her to feel left out." The fact that Jewel had never returned from her "bathroom" run wasn't lost on him. Jewel was rooting for him and he was sure that she was intentionally giving them space.

"I'll do that." Chloe looked at the door again before sitting back.

"It's been a while. I don't think she's coming back," Donovan responded to Chloe's constant looking back toward the hotel.

"Maybe I should go check on her. She did have quite a few of those rum cocktails."

Donovan stood. "Come on." He held his hand out. "I'll walk you to your suite."

Chloe looked at him for a moment before taking his outstretched hand. A quick current shot through him when their palms touched. Donovan liked it. He wondered if she felt it, too, and if she did, had she enjoyed it as much as he had?

Helping Chloe to her feet, he held on until she tamed her billowing dress from the gusty ocean breeze. Donovan deliberately slowed to an unhurried stride as they made their way into the hotel. Remembering his former years, he chuckled.

"What's so funny?" Chloe asked.

"Did you know I had a crush on you back in high school?"

Chloe's mouth fell open. "Really?"

"Yeah!"

"I never would have thought that, especially with all those girls that hung around you and your brother all of the time."

"Those were just friends." Donovan dismissed her comment with a flick of his hand.

"Yeah, right. Friends with benefits I'm sure."

Donovan's reply was a hearty laugh. "Maybe," he finally said. He couldn't deny the truth. As a star basketball player, he always had a healthy following of girls vying for his attention. "You always seemed so mature back then."

"People always said that. I think it's that oldest-child thing. I had to watch over my siblings and be the responsible one."

"That's not always fun," Donovan said.

They had reached the door to the resort. Chloe paused with a faraway look in her eyes. "Sometimes I resented always being the responsible one." She shook her head. "I missed out on a lot of fun."

"It's never too late," Donovan said. Chloe shrugged as she walked through the door while Donovan held it open. "There's no better time than the present."

"I'm too old for that stuff now." Chloe waved off his notion, continuing toward the elevator.

"You've always played it safe, huh?"

Chloe responded with a nod.

"No wonder I never saw you at the parties."

"I bet you saw Jewel there." Donovan nodded, confirming her suspicion, and Chloe tittered. "I remember her sneaking out her bedroom window. She hasn't changed much, you know."

"Oh, I know." Donovan raised a brow and pressed the call button for the elevator.

They continued reminiscing about the years behind them, reaching her hotel suite far too soon. They stood silently for a moment.

"Are we on for dinner tomorrow?" Donovan leaned against the wall.

"I'll let you know for sure tomorrow. Is that okay?"

"Not a problem." Donovan leaned forward and kissed her cheek as if it was the most natural thing. "See you soon," he said after she opened the door. "Good night, Jewel," he said loud enough for her to hear from the hallway.

"Good night, Don," Jewel yelled back.

Taking in the surprised look on Chloe's face, Donovan grinned, winked and headed down the hall back toward the elevator. It was apparent that Chloe was the last to realize that Jewel truly did leave them alone on purpose.

Donovan was thankful for her intuition. He looked forward to spending more time with Chloe the next evening. Jewel's actions tonight let him know he had an ally and he planned to use her help to satisfy his curiosity about Chloe.

Chapter 5

"Jewel!" Chloe shrieked when she had closed the hotel room door behind her. Jewel tucked her head into her shoulders and giggled. "You just left me out there by myself?"

"You weren't by yourself. Donovan was there," Jewel said matter-of-factly. She closed her laptop, got up from the desk and lay across the couch.

"You know what I mean." Chloe rolled her eyes and sucked her teeth. She wasn't really mad at Jewel, she just wished she'd given her a heads-up about leaving her alone with Donovan. "You could have said you weren't coming back out."

Jewel flopped on the couch, hit the mute button on the remote and faced Chloe. "Then you would have tried to come with me. Did you have a nice conversation?"

Chloe sat on the sofa, fixing a narrowed gaze on Jewel. "What made you think I wanted to be alone with him?"

"I knew that he wanted to be alone with you. You should have seen the way he stared when you started singing. That man was mesmerized. I thought he had fallen in love right then and there." Jewel sat up suddenly. "Did you know he had a crush on you when we were in high school?"

"He told me tonight. How'd you know?" Chloe parked one hand on her hip. Everyone seemed to know what was going on except her.

"He asked me to hook the two of you up back then. I told him not to waste his time because you wouldn't be interested."

"Why'd you say that?"

"You weren't rebellious enough to go against mom's orders. I knew there was no way you were going to date him. You hardly push back against her now and you're almost thirty."

"None of that's true. Mom doesn't run my life, nor am I that close to thirty!"

Jewel threw her head back and laughed. "You're on the other side of twenty-five. That's close enough!"

Chloe tossed a pillow at Jewel. She caught the pillow, twisted her lips and looked at Chloe sideways before laughing.

"Whatever." Chloe paused a moment and then went on to explain herself. "I tried to be an example for you all," she said, referring to her siblings. "I always felt like I needed to protect the three of you."

Jewel sat up, looked at Chloe and sighed. "And we appreciated it, but, sis, we're all grown now. I just want you to be bold enough to live on your own terms for once in your life."

Chloe huffed. "I do live on my own terms." She didn't sound convincing even to herself.

"You never answered my question," Jewel reminded her.

"What question?" Chloe was puzzled.

"Did you have a nice conversation?"

Chloe shrugged. "He asked me to dinner."

Jewel's eyes widened and so did her smile. "You said yes, right?"

"I told him that I'd let him know. I don't want to leave you hanging."

"Oh. Don't worry about me. I'll be fine. Tell him you'll go."

"It would be nice. We had a great time tonight, but part

of me wants to go because he's a cool guy and the other part feels like I shouldn't bother."

Jewel whipped her head in Chloe's direction. "Why not?"

"Why start something that won't go anywhere?"

"Who said it won't go anywhere? Who even cares if it goes anywhere? Just have a good time." Jewel waved away Chloe's concerned look. Jewel held her hand up. "And please do not say it's because our mothers wouldn't approve because I don't want to hear that!"

"Then I won't say it." Chloe shrugged, pulled pajamas from her suitcase and started toward the bathroom. She didn't realize that Jewel had tossed the pillow back at her until she felt it against her back.

"You better go to dinner with that man," Jewel yelled after Chloe as she entered the bathroom.

Squeezing a swirl of face wash in her hands, Chloe thought about what taking Donovan up on his offer for dinner meant.

She enjoyed his company and couldn't deny that she was curious about who Donovan really was. If it weren't for their problematic family history, would she consider seriously dating Donovan? Her answer was an unwavering yes. Who wouldn't? Donovan was handsome, successful and seemed to have a great personality. The only questionable issue was the fact that the Rivers brothers were known to be ladies' men and Chloe had never been into players.

Chloe continued to ponder scenarios pertaining to Donovan as she showered. After all that careful consideration, she wondered why she bothered thinking so hard. He had only asked her to dinner, not for her hand in marriage. How harmful could dinner be?

Chloe stepped out the shower, wrapped a large plush towel around her body and went to tell Jewel that she'd decided to go to dinner.

Jewel was sprawled across the bed asleep with the TV blaring and all the lights on. Chloe shook her head, turned off the lights in Jewel's room and prepared for bed herself. They had another long day ahead of them.

An hour passed and Chloe lay in the bed still awake. Sleep evaded her while her mind churned with thoughts of how this dinner with Donovan would turn out.

He'd kissed her on the cheek but she thought nothing of it, considering it a friendly gesture. By the time she finally fell asleep, she'd fully convinced herself that there was nothing wrong with having a friendly dinner. In fact, she looked forward to it. She was on a beautiful tropical island and even though she was there for business, she was determined to play as much as she worked for a change.

Her sister's comment taunted her as well. Chloe had to agree, it was time for her to be rebellious enough to live aloud. She no longer had to set examples for her younger siblings. They were all adults. It was time for her to have some fun.

Despite little sleep, Chloe woke energized and more excited about having dinner with Donovan than she was willing to admit. Feeling giddy, she hummed as she dressed, took extra care with her hair as she delicately brushed it.

"You sound chipper this morning." Chloe was so caught up in her own elation that Jewel's comment startled her.

"What's that supposed to mean?"

Jewel fluttered her hand. "Since when do you hum and sing while you're getting dressed?" She chuckled. "You're excited about your date tonight, aren't you?"

"No!" Chloe shook her head as she dismissed Jewel's observation. "And it's not a date. We're just having dinner." She spread another coat of lip gloss across her lips and through the reflection in the mirror, she caught Jewel cutting her eyes toward the ceiling. After a moment she confessed. "Okay, maybe I'm a little excited."

Jewel ran over and hugged her. "Yay! Chloe's gonna have some fun tonight." She swayed her hips, dancing out her own excitement. "Enjoy yourself." She straightened her back and pointed her finger as if it were a command. "Don't think about anything or anyone back home. You hear me? And let him kiss you at the end of the night if he wants to. Who's going to know?"

"You will, Ms. Big Mouth."

"I'll only tell Jade. She has to know."

"Jewel!"

"What?" Jewel unsuccessfully tried to refrain from snickering. She fluffed Chloe's shoulder-length hair with her fingers. "Let me do your makeup tonight. Oh! Let's go shopping around lunchtime and find a nice dress for later."

"Jewel. Slow down. It's not that serious." Chloe looked back at her.

"Oh, but it's fun! Besides, who needs a serious reason to shop?"

Chloe closed her eyes and exhaled.

"Now get out of the bathroom so I can take my shower." Jewel turned on the shower water.

Chloe gathered her comb and cosmetics that lay sprawled across the vanity top and stuffed them in her travel bag. "It's all yours," she said, exiting the bathroom.

Chloe couldn't remember the last time she'd been on a date. Placing her toiletry bag inside her carry-on, she imagined how tonight would go.

Envisioning a moonlit light dinner accompanied by a tropical soundtrack of waves crashing against the shore made her smile. A shiver crawled up her hand where she imagined him touching her. Then she chided herself for acting like a lovesick teenager.

She thought about her sister's comment. If Donovan tried to kiss her tonight, would she let him?

Chapter 6

Excitement surged through Donovan. The conference was going well for him but that's not what caused him to feel so elated. He looked forward to his date with Chloe. Looking down at his watch made him smile. He had several hours to go before meeting up with Chloe.

Donovan thought about his crush on Chloe. High school was a long time ago. Since then, he'd been the target of many women's desire. He couldn't pinpoint what it was about Chloe that intrigued him then or now but he intended to enjoy the process of finding out. Hearing her beautiful voice during karaoke caused his sense of curiosity to leap off the meter. He'd felt her soul when she sang.

Thankfully, the rest of the afternoon sailed by quickly. Donovan hurried to his room, showered and returned to the bar in the hotel's lobby dressed in a blue lightweight sports jacket, white linen shirt and slacks. He topped his look with a straw fedora in the same tan hue of his pants.

A pre-dinner cocktail was the perfect way to start the evening. He'd given Chloe some extra time to do all the stuff women do to get ready to go out. After his drink, he called her.

"Hey there! We're meeting in the lobby, right?" She answered out of breath.

"How about we meet at the bar by the pool?" Donovan heard her groan. "Are you okay?"

Chloe huffed. "Yes. I was just turning everything upside down looking for my sandal." She chuckled. "I promise you I'm not out of shape, just rushing. That's all."

"Your shape seems fine to me," he joked.

Silence.

Donovan expected a laugh but then wondered if he'd offended her. "I was joking."

"I know." There was more silence. "It's fine. I'll be down in a few minutes." Chloe hung up before Donovan could say anything else.

Chloe was going to have to get used to his sense of humor. He planned to take his time getting to know her. Something told him she was worth it.

Donovan headed to the pool bar, ordered another glass of Cabernet and looked out over the convention crowd who had now traded in their business casual garb for more relaxed options, like shorts and swimsuits. Boisterous laughter ran out amongst a group of gentlemen mixing with the loud merengue streaming from hidden speakers. Several flat-screen TVs hung from the rafters, adding an array of voices and volume to the clanging of plates and utensils.

This symphony would continue through most of the night, which was why Donovan opted for a more serene environment for his date with Chloe.

His Cabernet arrived just as he spotted Chloe stepping off the elevator. She arrested his attention in a flowing coral maxi dress that slightly swept the floor beneath her and exposed the smooth skin of her shoulders. Her hair was pulled up in a bun with a few delicate wisps hanging down around her face.

The heads of several men turned to her as she made her way toward him. A cocky grin eased across his lips, proud of the fact that the center of the many patrons' attention was his date for the night. As she drew closer, he quickly took in her long lashes, high cheekbones and the soft pink sheen on her lips.

He stood, greeting her with a peck on the cheek and a possessive hand placed respectfully in the small of her back.

"Ready to go?" he asked.

"Yes." Her affirmation was followed by a sweet smile that Donovan wished he could have caught on camera.

Leaving his wine behind, Donovan swept his hand before her, allowing her to walk ahead of him, eager to begin his night out. "Oh!" He stopped. Chloe turned to him. "About my little joke earlier, I hope I didn't offend you."

Chloe waved her hand. "I wasn't offended." She pursed her lips. "And I'm sure the pun was intended."

"Indeed it was." Donovan laughed. "So we're all good?"

"All good."

"Great. I don't want to scare you off on the first date."

"I'm a big girl, Donovan." Chloe laughed and shook her head.

"Let's go have some fun then." Donovan took Chloe by the hand and led her through the resort.

After a brief inquiry with the concierge, they hopped in a taxi. At first, Chloe quietly took in the tropical scenery as they drove along the main road.

"By the way," he began, capturing her attention. "You look absolutely beautiful." He couldn't help touching a wisp of hair that hung by her ear.

Chloe blushed, dipping her head into her shoulders. "Thank you."

Donovan enjoyed watching her blush. To him, it meant that his compliment affected her in some way.

"So where are we going?" she asked as she turned to him.

"A place a friend told me about. I think you're going to like it."

Light conversation carried them the rest of the way to the restaurant. The taxi pulled up to an exquisite modern structure, which rivaled anything in an upscale design magazine. A stone pathway nestled in the center of lush tropical flora led them to the front entrance of the establishment.

Donovan announced his name and the host led him up a winding staircase to a rooftop seating area that overlooked the ocean. A live band played near the center of the room before a cozy dance floor.

The host pulled out chairs for both, giving them a perfect view of the water. Donovan sat, removed his hat and placed it on his leg.

Chloe looked around and nodded approvingly. "This is a beautiful place. You should thank your friend."

Their waiter quickly approached, took drink orders and left them to their small talk. Donovan was anxious to make Chloe feel comfortable so he could dine with the magnetic woman that sang karaoke the other night.

"Are you okay?" he asked.

"Yeah…" She seemed to want to say more. Donovan waited, giving her space to find her words. "It's been a long time since I've been on a…date."

"Really?" Donovan reared his head back slightly. "A beautiful woman like you?"

Chloe's cheeks flushed. A coy smile told Donovan that she appreciated his compliments. "Yes. I've been buried in work and time just passed by. It wasn't intentional. I just enjoy my work."

"So what exactly do you do for Chandler Food Corp?"

Donovan seemed to have asked the right question. Chloe's expression brightened as she talked about both sides of their family's business. It was clear that she had a passion for planning the extravagant events that their waterside venue, Chandlers, was known for. She spoke highly of their plans for expansion and of all the work they'd put into increasing their visibility across the Gold Coast.

Her excitement engaged him. She asked him about his work with his family's catering hall. He shared a little family history, telling the charming story about how the name La Belle Riviere came about. His father endearingly referred to his mother as his beautiful half as opposed to using the more common term, his better half.

"Aw." Chloe inclined her head sideways and pouted. "How sweet."

They exhausted the topic of work over a few glasses of wine before it turned more personal.

"So about this crush." Chloe swirled the liquid in her wine glass and chuckled.

"Ha! Those were the days." Donovan took a sip, leaning to the side so the waiter could place the hot plate piled with an impressive lobster that was still steaming. He waited until her plate of sea bass was set on the table before continuing. "I'm surprised you didn't know about it back then."

"It's amazing how we were so close, yet so far from each other. Other than seeing you and your siblings in school and around the community, I really don't know much about you guys." Chloe took in a forkful of her dish and sighed, indicating her approval of the meal.

"Good…huh?" Donovan asked, pausing between his words.

"Delicious!" Chloe covered her mouth as she spoke.

Donovan tilted his head. "What would you like to know about me?" he asked, bringing the conversation back to them. His voice dipped lower than he'd intended.

Chloe sat back and shrugged her shoulders. "I don't know." After a moment, she added, "Let's start from the beginning?"

"I was born…"

"Not that far back, silly," she interjected and then laughed.

Donovan snickered. "Did you know that I still play the tenor sax?" he said, dipping a chunk of lobster meat into the butter sauce.

Chloe swallowed the sip of wine she'd just taken before speaking. "I remember that from prep school."

"Yes, I play with some friends in the city sometimes. There's a lounge that books us for gigs."

"You're part of a band? Very cool! How often?" she asked.

"Yes. Quite often, actually," Donovan said matter-of-factly.

"I'd love to hear you play one day," she said.

"We can arrange that when we get back home." Donovan paused a moment, but continued when Chloe didn't respond to his invitation. "What about you? Hobbies?"

"I haven't indulged much, but as you know, I like to sing."

"And that you do very well." Chloe blushed. Donovan smiled. "What else?"

"Um." Chloe looked up as if the answer were on the ceiling. "I like to play chess."

"Really!" Donovan's eyes stretched. He was genuinely surprised.

"I'm quite good at it, too," she proclaimed.

"We'll have to see about that." Donovan sat back confidently.

Chloe narrowed her gaze at him. "Maybe we should engage in a game one day."

"I have to warn you. I play quite well."

"I guess we will have to see who's better." Chloe leaned back and crossed her arms.

"You're challenging me." Donovan sat erect and pointed to his own chest.

"If you think you can handle getting beat by a lady like me," Chloe stated and dared him with a direct stare before sipping her wine.

Placing both elbows on the table, Donovan leaned closer to Chloe. "I'll set the place, you set the time," he said.

Chloe fell into a fit of laughter. "I pulled you right into that one."

"Oh no! You're not getting out of this. We have a chess match coming up."

"We only have another day or so here in Puerto Rico."

"We don't have to play here." Donovan waited to see how she would respond to him alluding to seeing her back home. Once again, she left his statement hanging.

By then, Chloe seemed to have entered her comfort zone. They finished dinner, then shared a decadent dessert and talked some more. Conversation flowed easily, dipping in and out of past years and springing forward into future hopes and dreams.

"Why don't you sing more often?"

Chloe lowered her eyes and swirled the wine in her glass again. Donovan noted that as a gesture of avoidance.

"I just don't have time for it. I work so many hours."

Seeing that the subject slightly changed her mood, Donovan wanted to recover the moment. "Let's dance."

"Sure."

Donovan stood, placed his hat on the empty seat beside him and held out his hand. Chloe placed hers in his. Donovan two-stepped a version of salsa to the dance floor. Once there, he turned to Chloe, held out one hand and put the other gently against her lower back.

For a moment, they stood staring eye-to-eye before Donovan began swaying his hips in time with the upbeat tempo. Pulled in by her eyes and delicate long lashes,

Donovan didn't want to look away. He held her gaze until it intensified slightly. Chloe was the first to break the connection but not before he felt something spark between them.

Dancing in sync, they found their collaborative rhythm. Donovan led, guiding their movements to match the syncopated tempo. Songs started and ended until it seemed like one long refrain.

Chloe folded her body into his. He released her with a turn. Catching the beat, they stepped in time to the spirited beat until Donovan felt a bead of sweat roll down the center of his back. The longer they danced, the more he pulled her in. Dancing chest to chest caused heat to circle in his groin. This warmth had nothing to do with the fact that they'd been moving nonstop for a while now. This heat was directly linked to Donovan's growing desire for the woman skillfully twirling her hips against him. He needed air.

"Wanna go outside?" he asked. Chloe nodded and then delicately wiped a bead of sweat from her brow. Holding her hand, Donovan led the way to the balcony, welcoming the cooling ocean breeze. "Are you enjoying yourself?"

"Am I?" Chloe asked breathlessly, wiping her brow once again. "I haven't had this much fun in so long. Thanks."

Donovan's response was a smile. He looked out over the water, listening to the hollow sound of the waves. Still holding her hand, they stood silently on the terrace, allowing the gentle wind to lick away the sweat generated from their sensual dance. Rays of moonlight bobbled on the water, inviting Donovan to the shore.

"Let's go," he whispered to Chloe, paid the bill and led her through the restaurant to the exit facing the sea.

Donovan removed his shoes and rolled the hem of his pants just above his ankles. Chloe followed suit, removing her sandals and knotting the end of her dress below her knees. Hand-in-hand, they walked where the water met the sand. Chloe's hand felt good in his, as if it belonged. They stopped walking, still holding hands, and turned to watch the evening's light dance across the ripples in the midnight blue water.

A fleeting thought about settling down flashed across Donovan's mind and he snickered to himself. It was too early to consider all of that but he certainly looked forward to exploring more of her world. He wondered about her dreams.

"What's one thing that you've always wanted to do?"

"Hmm." Chloe sighed and closed her eyes, stayed that way for a moment and opened them back up. Instead of answering, she smiled and shrugged her shoulders.

"What was the first thing that came to mind?" Donovan turned to her, studying her pensive gaze.

"As a little girl, I used to imagine singing before an adoring crowd and receiving a standing ovation. I'd stand in the mirror, throwing kisses to my fans and telling them how much I love them, the way Diana Ross used to do." She giggled. "Sounds silly, right?"

"That can still happen."

"Oh, please!" Chloe dismissed the notion with a wave of her hand. "That was a little girl's fantasy."

Donovan observed her closely. After a moment she looked away, directing her attention toward her feet. He watched her create abstract swirls in the sand with her bare toes. Donovan felt as if there were more she wanted to say.

"What about you?" she asked after a while.

Donovan chuckled. "When I was a kid, I fantasized about being an astronaut."

"What happened?"

"Girls," Donovan said matter-of-factly. Both enjoyed a good chuckle.

He liked the way she laughed: the way her head fell

back revealing the sexy long line of her neck, the sweet melody she released into the air, the way she wrinkled her nose and how her sweetheart lips parted. Suddenly, he felt the urge to kiss those lips.

Chloe stopped laughing and looked at him curiously when she noticed him watching her. "What?" she asked, staring inquisitively.

"I want to take you out again." He was direct.

"Let me check with my sister to see what her plans are for tomorrow."

"I'm talking about when we get back home to Long Island. I want to *see* you on a regular basis." A few dates wouldn't satisfy him. He was interested in the quest. Where could this go?

Chloe tucked her lips in but didn't say a word. Donovan imagined her doing the same thing when he made that comment earlier when they were on the phone. He was beginning to understand the indications of her silence.

"I love my mother but she doesn't run my life." Donovan faced her, taking both her hands into his. He looked into her eyes. After a moment she looked away. "I want to see you again." It was more than a statement.

Chloe's only response was a sigh and a smile. Donovan wasn't settling for "no" as an answer. Getting what he wanted had never been a concern. He only ever needed to figure out how to attain that which he desired.

Chapter 7

Jewel pulled the door to the hotel suite open before Chloe could remove the keycard.

"What—"

"I heard you put the card in the door. Come on!" Jewel pulled Chloe into the suite. "Tell me all about it." Jewel smiled hard and wide. "Did you kiss him?"

Jewel flopped on the couch in the living room and sat cross-legged. She kept her eyes trained on Chloe as she kicked off her shoes and unknotted the bottom of her dress. Jewel's eyes were wide with anticipation. The only thing missing was a bowl of popcorn. "Tell me you kissed him," she prompted.

"No, we didn't kiss, but we did hold hands."

Jewel's mouth formed an O and her shoulders slumped. "You've been out with him all this time." She craned her head toward the digital clock on the desk in the living area. "And you didn't even get a kiss? You held hands?" she asked incredulously.

Chloe went into the bathroom on her side of the suite and started the shower. The heat of their dance, mixed with the salty beach air, made her feel sticky. Jewel hopped off the bed and followed Chloe when she came back into the room.

"So tell me about the date," Jewel urged.

Chloe grabbed a T-strapped nightie, turned back toward the bathroom and bumped right into Jewel.

"Oh my goodness, Jewel. Give me some space!" Chloe couldn't help but laugh.

"Ha!" Jewel hooted, making Chloe giggle some more.

When they gathered themselves, Chloe began to tell Jewel's eager ears how much she enjoyed Donovan's company. Jewel closed the lid of the commode, covered it with a towel and sat down, listening to Chloe as she showered.

"Wow! So what's next?"

"Pass me a towel," Chloe said. Jewel did as she was asked. "I don't know what's next." Chloe patted her body dry, wrapped the towel around her and left the bathroom with Jewel on her heels.

"You don't want to see him again?"

Chloe flopped on the couch and huffed. "I do but…"

"But what?" Jewel planted her hands on her hips.

"You know…" Jewel twisted her lips. Chloe grunted. "I just don't want any drama."

"Chloe." Jewel sat beside her sister. "For once, forget about doing what you think you're 'supposed' to do." Jewel curled her fingers into quotes. "And do what feels good to Chloe."

Jewel's words brought Chloe back to the question Donovan asked on the beach. *What's one thing that you've always wanted to do?*

Donovan had no idea how loaded that question was. It would have taken more time than they had for her to tell the truth. She'd backed herself into a highly safe box in life. She had long ago begun to feel caged and compelled to break out of the safe zone she'd created, knowing that her actions might shock some and anger others. However, every day, she longed to break free.

"It's obvious that you like him and he likes you. You're a brilliant, talented, hardworking woman and you deserve to indulge every now and then. Go out with the man. No one ever said that the two of you have to get married. When the novelty wears off, you both can go your separate ways and no one will be any wiser—except me of course. Ha!" Jewel slapped her knee, mimicking an instinctive gesture of one of their favorite uncles.

"Uncle Jack!" they said at the same time and burst into laughter.

"I don't know what I want to do," Chloe began when they calmed down. "I need to think about this."

Jewel stood and headed toward her bed. "Good. And remember to focus on what *you* want. Don't worry about anyone else." Jewel lay down but jumped up almost immediately. "Wait!" she said, running through the suite. "I have to tell you about the guy I met in the lobby. He's from New York."

Jewel sat on the edge of Chloe's bed and shared a witty rendition of her encounter with a tall, dark and handsome man from the hotel restaurant industry. As usual, he was eating from the palm of her hand by the time she left him. They'd exchanged contact information but Jewel wasn't sure if she'd pursue him any further since he seemed too straight-laced for her liking.

"You're too much." Chloe slipped under the covers. "See you in the morning." She went to sleep with mirth in her spirit and Donovan on her mind.

The next morning she rose to an endearing text from Donovan noting that he'd had a great evening. Chloe wondered about Jewel, who was probably still sleeping, and pulled back the covers. As her feet hit the floor, her cell phone rang.

"Good morning." Chloe was surprised by the smile in her own voice.

"Good morning. Have you two had breakfast yet?" Donovan's voice seemed as smooth and rich as molasses.

"Actually, we're just getting up," she said, yawning and stretching. "Oh! Excuse me. Let me check with my sister." Chloe stuffed her feet into her slippers, swished her way to Jewel's room, and sat on the side of her bed. "Jewel! Hey, Jewel. Wake up," she sang.

"Whaaa…" Jewel whined and pulled the covers over her head.

"Get up. Donovan is asking if we've had breakfast."

Jewel groaned. "What time is it?"

Chloe looked at the clock on the table. "Eight thirty-six."

"Darnit!" Jewel pushed the covers off. "There was a session I wanted to make at nine." She swung her legs over the side of the bed. "It doesn't look like that's going to happen now. Breakfast sounds great."

"We're good for breakfast," Chloe said to Donovan.

"Meet me in the lobby by nine thirty. I have a great place."

"You got it." Chloe ended the call and hopped up. After speaking with Donovan, she felt energized.

Chloe headed to the bathroom. Jewel dragged herself to the one connected to her room. Within the hour, they were dressed and stepping off the elevator to meet Donovan.

Chloe spotted Donovan near the entrance with his cell phone glued to his ear. As they approached, Donovan wrapped up his call and smiled. Chloe could tell the smile was somewhat forced.

"Good morning, ladies. You look beautiful!" Donovan gave Jewel a friendly peck on the cheek before leaning toward Chloe. Donovan took one of her hands in his, placed the other on her arm and pressed his lips against her cheek, lingering just longer than what could be considered friendly.

Chloe's cheeks burned from blushing but the spot where his lips had just been tingled. She swore she could hear the actual sizzle from the sparks that passed through her when his lips touched her face. Jewel discreetly raised her brows and grinned.

"Shall we go?" he asked, holding both elbows out. The sisters hooked their arms in his and headed for the door.

Donovan had done it again, Chloe thought as they pulled up to another beautiful establishment. Donovan paid the driver and advised that he'd call him back when they were ready to be picked up.

The restaurant was its own tropical paradise. The interior was elegant, complete with water fountains and lush tropical plants with a bright nautical theme. Delectable aromas met them at the door, inviting them in.

A young hostess guided them to a table on the deck overlooking a marina. Chloe watched the boats bob on top of the water. The cool breeze caressed her skin and lifted her shoulder-length hair.

Their server arrived promptly and took their orders. He moved in a stealth-like manner as he delivered their drinks and meals. It was as if he could read their minds. Chloe thought about wanting more water, looked at her glass and found it full. The only thing better than the impeccable service was Donovan's presence. Jewel's spirited demeanor was a plus as well.

"Do you like sailing?" Donovan asked Chloe. He looked out over the marina.

"Yes. Unfortunately, I can't remember the last time I was on a boat."

"That's because you don't take time off," Jewel said. When she finished her forkful of eggs, she continued. "Remember when Dad used to take us out on the boat when we were kids?" Jewel questioned and took a sip of her mimosa.

"My goodness! I used to love that." Chloe smiled as she reminisced. "What about you, Donovan? You sail?" Chloe pushed her half-eaten vegetable omelet aside and picked up one of the mini breakfast pastries that were delectably perched on a long white dish. She took a bite and closed her eyes momentarily, savoring the taste. At her reaction, Jewel reached for one as well.

"I sure do. It was one of my dad's favorite things to do also. My brother and I try to get out on the water a couple times a year." Donovan stopped speaking for a moment and held Chloe in his gaze. She felt it, only responded with an inward smile. "What are some other things you enjoy, Chloe?"

Chloe tilted her head and narrowed her eyes thoughtfully.

"Chloe is a mixed bag," Jewel interjected, holding her hand over her mouth to cover the pastry she'd just bit into. Chloe shook her head and laughed, assuming she hadn't answered quickly enough for her sister. "It depends on her mood. Only lately, she hasn't done much of anything besides work. Just so you know, she's the type that can go from the bowling alley to the boardroom. It depends on what she's in the mood for. When she's feeling adventurous, she'll jump out of a plane and other times, she's happy sitting on the couch, eating a bowl of popcorn while watching movies."

"My kind of girl!" Donovan said.

Chloe had never blushed more in her life. "Thanks. I am pretty well rounded," she said confidently.

"Oh! And she plays a hell of a game of chess." Jewel took a long sip of water to wash down the dessert.

"I've heard about that. I need to see that for myself," Donovan said, inviting himself to the challenge.

"Anytime, my friend. I haven't slaughtered a good-looking man at chess in a long time." Chloe laughed as soon as she said those flirtatious words.

Jewel's brows rose and so did Donovan's. Chloe held up her glass of mimosa, her third since they'd arrived, and looked at it as if there was something in the glass that caused such audacious speech. Despite being a little embarrassed, her forwardness made her feel giddy.

"I'd be happy to take you up on that challenge if you think I qualify." Donovan tucked his luscious lips inside his mouth and licked them—a gesture that Chloe deemed extremely sexy.

"Oh, you qualify!" She laughed aloud. Jewel's eyes stretched and she looked back and forth between Donovan and Chloe.

Donovan sipped his mimosa, without taking his eyes off Chloe. Usually she'd match his gaze for a moment and look away, but this time, she refused to break the stare. Unspoken desires seemed to pass between them, intensifying the moment and charging the atmosphere.

"Good, because I don't think I've ever been challenged by such a beautiful woman before. This will be interesting I'm sure." Donovan raised his glass, nodding his acceptance. Chloe raised her glass, sealing the deal.

Jewel cleared her throat. "I'm still here. Should I just leave you two alone?" She chuckled, causing them to join her.

Chloe looked at her watch. "Oh! I really need to get back. I can't miss my lunch meeting." She was surprised at how much time had passed. Chloe enjoyed the company, energy and the conversation and hated that it was coming to an end.

Donovan signaled for the waiter. When he got his attention, he wiggled his hand, indicating that he was ready for the check.

"When are you heading back home?" Donovan asked.

"The day after tomorrow. We're on the first flight out," Jewel stated.

"Me, too. Perhaps we could ride to the airport together,"

Donovan said, taking the billfold from the waiter and stuffing his credit card inside.

"We could," Chloe answered, batting her eyes. Who knew flirting could be so much fun? "What are you doing for dinner tonight?" Chloe tilted her head and raised her shoulders playfully.

Donovan's sexy smile eased across his lips again. "I was hoping you'd join me wherever I go."

"Gladly." Chloe had always been confident but was surprised at her own forwardness. It was almost like an out-of-body experience but it felt real and amazing and exciting. "See you tonight."

Donovan winked as he accepted the billfold with the receipt, signed his name, and handed it back to the waiter. "Time for work." Donovan pressed his hands into the table and stood. "Jewel, you're welcome to join us tonight."

"No, thanks." Jewel placed her napkin on the table and stood also. "The two of you forgot I was here just now. Ha! Enjoy yourselves tonight. Don't worry about me. I know how to keep myself company."

"Sorry, sis." Chloe frowned once she was on her feet.

"No worries. I planned to sip on a few cocktails by the pool." Jewel waved off her concern.

"Then it's a date?" Donovan asked.

"It's a date," Chloe confirmed.

Donovan gestured for Jewel to walk ahead of him and then placed his hand on the small of Chloe's back, guiding her toward the door as well.

Chloe had a long day ahead of her and wondered if she would be able to successfully absorb any information. She felt that pushing thoughts of Donovan aside throughout the day would prove challenging. She was already putting her outfit together for her next evening out with Donovan. Now that she was much more comfortable in his presence—with or without cocktail fuel—she looked forward to spending more time with him.

Maybe tonight she'd even let him kiss her. Perhaps she might even initiate the kiss. *Hmmm.* What a thought.

Chapter 8

Chloe wasn't happy. Donovan could tell by the sound of her voice. He'd been so caught up in her flirting the day before that he had completely forgotten about an important dinner meeting. When he had called her last night to cancel, she'd sounded dejected but seemed to understand. He'd asked her to meet him for after-dinner cocktails, but the meeting lasted longer than he anticipated. He'd texted her when it was over. She hadn't responded. This morning, she answered his text and he released a breath that felt as if he'd been holding it for hours.

This would be their last day in Puerto Rico and he wanted to make it up to her before they left the island. He hoped that what he had planned would work out.

Donovan knocked on Chloe's room door, wondering how she and her sister would respond to the liberties he'd taken to plan the day out.

Jewel opened the door and peeked through a small crack. "Donovan?" She rubbed her eyes and stretched them wide.

"It's me. Are you decent in there?" He leaned against the doorframe.

"Not yet. Chloe's still in the shower." Jewel groaned. Donovan imagined her stretching on the opposite side of the door.

"Good. We're playing hooky today!" He smiled, awaiting her response.

"Huh?" Jewel peeked around the edge of the door, revealing more of her face. She raised one brow.

Donovan repeated his statement in the most nonchalant manner.

"Sounds great. I'll let her know," Jewel said, revealing a tad bit of excitement. Either she had a late night or she simply wasn't a morning person, Donovan surmised.

"I mean all three of us. I want you to come with us so you don't miss the fun."

"Fun?" Jewel perked up even more. "Oh, I love fun."

Donovan was glad to have Jewel's support. Now he had to make sure that Chloe was open to his idea. "Do you ladies have any important meetings that I need to consider?"

"We'll adjust. Both of us could use the break. Give us thirty minutes." Jewel went to close the door but stuck her head back out. "Wait! How should we dress?"

"Comfortably. Shorts would be good. I've planned a bit of adventure. Bring a bathing suit and meet me in the lobby."

"Woo!" Jewel raised one fist before pushing the door closed. She let out a few more hoots.

Donovan laughed, listening to Jewel's antics through the closed door. He heard her call out to Chloe before her voice faded.

Exiting the elevator, Donovan walked right through the lobby into the bright morning sun. Postcards couldn't appropriately capture the beauty of the landscape, sand and magnificent blue of the pristine sea. The scene affected his mood. He felt lighter now than he had when he got up.

Calling in the favors he'd had on hold, Donovan confirmed all of the reservations for the day. He was confident that with Jewel's encouragement, Chloe wouldn't object to spending the day with him. He wanted to spend this time with Chloe and didn't want to leave Jewel out. She'd been supportive of his attempts to get closer to Chloe.

Once he was finished on the phone, Donovan sat in a lounger alongside the pool. Lying back, he soaked up some morning sun. After a while, Donovan spotted the girls coming his way. Both were dressed elegantly casual. Jewel looked nice, but Donovan couldn't take his eyes off the long, smooth legs that gracefully carried Chloe closer to him.

He could see her white bikini top through her sheer cover-up. The bottom of it met the hem of her shorts. Her floppy beach hat dipped on one side, while the other revealed the rims of her designer sunglasses.

"Good morning, ladies." Donovan stood to greet them. Again, he allowed his embrace and friendly peck on Chloe's cheek to linger.

"Morning, Donovan." Chloe offered up a cordial smile.

"Hey, Don," Jewel said, shortening his name and shielding her shaded eyes from the glare of the sun.

"I'm glad you decided to join me," he said to both ladies. "Again, I'm sorry about last night." He directed his apology toward Chloe.

"It's no problem, Donovan. Business is what we're here for."

"Thanks for understanding. We need to get going."

Donovan beamed as he led the ladies through the lobby to a car waiting for them in the resort's bay. The driver opened the door and the three climbed in. Not long after, they arrived at their first stop where they enjoyed a delicious alfresco breakfast. The second stop was where the adventure began.

After riding up the mountainside by horseback, the three rappelled inside a deep cave where they explored the interior, led by an enthusiastic tour guide. At the next stop, they paddled through a glow-in-the-dark bioluminescent bay before zip-lining high above the treetops. A hearty lunch satisfied the ravenous appetites they worked up before relaxing on a private beach.

By the time they got back, the sun had begun to dip into the horizon. The three thrill-seekers resisted submitting to their worn bodies. Instead of taking naps, they took showers, producing a second wind.

Chloe returned to the lobby refreshed, adorned in a flowing maxi dresses. As they prepared to set sail on a chartered moonlight dinner-cruise, Jewel excused herself from the rest of their evening's activities.

"You two enjoy yourselves. I've got plans of my own for dinner." With a sly smile, Jewel tossed her hair and sauntered off. "Have fun!" she said without looking back.

Chloe and Donovan looked at each other for a moment and then laughed.

"That girl can amaze me." Chloe shook her head.

Although Donovan thoroughly enjoyed hanging with both sisters throughout the day, he looked forward to spending time alone with Chloe.

"That's Jewel," Donovan stated. "Now let's go finish up our night." Donovan took Chloe by the hand and led her to where their chartered yacht awaited them on the marina.

The sun had reserved the last of its orange glow for when they set sail. Chloe stood, holding the rail, looking over the water. Donovan posted closely behind her. For several moments, they simply enjoyed the breathtaking views and vibrant colors meeting along the horizon.

"Did I do okay?" Donovan whispered just behind her ear. He hadn't meant for his voice to sound so husky, but the floral scent wafting from her body had awakened his instincts.

"With what?" Chloe kept her eyes on the magical scenery.

"I wanted to make up for having to cancel dinner last night."

Chloe turned around. Facing Donovan with her back against the railing, their eyes met. He smiled, watching her eyes flit from side to side, searching his. She swallowed. He admired the curve of her neck, the heart-like shape of her lips, her elevated cheekbones and her doe eyes. Behind those eyes lay a hint of playfulness and an unconcealed measure of seduction.

The air around them sizzled. Both seemed to be arrested by the intensity of the other's gaze.

Chloe licked her lips. Donovan considered the gesture instinctive. It called out to him. Her moist lips were like an invitation. They compelled Donovan. He resisted for a moment, wanting to gauge her intent, not wanting to misread her actions. Yet, something pulled on him, like an unseen force. The desire to taste her lips overwhelmed him. He wanted to be a gentleman and acquire approval.

The atmosphere grew warm. His primal essence thumped in his core.

Donovan stepped closer to Chloe, reducing the space between them to a hair's width. Her lips parted. Donovan traced the bottom one with his finger. It trembled slightly and parted some more. He couldn't help himself. He heard her breath catch.

Cupping her cheeks in both his hands, he gently laid his lips on hers, pressed against them for a singular moment of sheer joy before coaxing her mouth wider. A warm sensation spread through him the instant their mouths connected. His core tightened.

The kiss became ravenous almost instantly. Chloe's hands were braced against his chest. She held on as if she needed him for balance. Her moan vibrated against his lips. He held on tighter. Kissed her deeper. Moved in closer.

The passion passing between them was explosive. They peeled themselves apart from one another in order to breathe but never let each other go. Donovan's eyes remained closed, savoring the sweet depths of her warm mouth. When he opened his eyes, he found hers still closed.

Examining her beautiful features, he pondered what it was about Chloe Chandler that compelled him. He wondered if this would be the last time he'd feel her lips against his.

Chapter 9

Chloe sat at the conference table across from the consultant who was going to work on their new marketing and PR campaign. She was all business since she'd hit the States. Flashbacks of her time with Donovan crept up at the most inopportune times, like now, but she was getting better at pushing them aside.

Though she hadn't physically seen him in the week that they'd been back, he showed up in her daydreams. They chatted by phone at night and texted by day, but Chloe was reluctant to move beyond that for several reasons. One, that kiss from their last night in Puerto Rico still managed to make her insides warm, and two, her mother El… Enough said.

"How do you plan to measure the results of the branding strategy?" Chloe asked the woman in the smart blue suit and brown shoulder-length hair. Kathy was her name and there was something ultra-cool about Kathy, Chloe thought. She'd liked what she and her partner Lynne had presented so far.

"I'm glad you asked." Kathy went on to explain the measurable aspects of the plan.

Chloe was used to the speech about other aspects of marketing not being guaranteed. She understood that well.

"Wait!" Chloe's mother, El, held her hand as high as her proverbial nose. "Did you say La Belle Riviere?" she asked Kathy. She had narrowed her eyes and pursed her lips when Kathy mentioned a successful component of another client's campaign that she'd planned to use with Chandlers. That client happened to be El's long-term nemesis and biggest competitor in the business.

"Yes. I imagine you're familiar with them. They run a very successful—"

El held her hand up again, interrupting Kathy's partner Lynne as she stood. "I think we're done here." She pressed imaginary wrinkles down the front of her elegantly styled designer dress. "Thank you for your time." She nodded politely as if she weren't dismissing them right in the middle of their proposal meeting.

Kathy and Lynne looked at each other and then El. Their shocked expressions finally landed on Chloe with knitted brows and questions lingering in their creased eyes.

"Excuse me, ladies. Mom, can I see you for a moment?" Chloe gently held her elbow and led her out of the conference room.

"Gladly." El sauntered toward the door in her four-inch heels. "Have a wonderful day, ladies. Thank you for your thorough presentation."

"Ma!" Chloe's words rushed past her lips in a hard whisper. She looked back into the conference room before turning her attention to her mother and continuing. "What was that?"

"We're not doing business with anyone doing business with that woman and her family."

Chloe's hand instinctively went to her forehead and she grunted. "Mom, are you serious? Aren't you the one who told me to never mix personal feelings with business?"

El straightened her back and chuckled. She looked at Chloe and shook her head as if she pitied her. "You see, darling, this is business. As our consultant, they will be provided access to some very confidential information. We can't have our competition become privy to any of that. There are more marketing firms in the region than theirs."

"They're the best. Their track record is unmatched."

"Humph." El dismissed Chloe, cutting her eyes. "There are plenty of other companies that are just as good."

Chloe dropped her shoulders. "You're making a mistake, Mom."

"I'm protecting our business. We can't afford to let our competition gain access to our strategies."

"That won't happen. These women are professionals and come highly recommended. Working with them will help us get the results we've been seeking, more visibility and younger clients."

"She just told us about one of their successful campaigns. I don't want out business discussed with other clients like that."

Chloe took a deep breath, trying to rein in her annoyance. She'd never gone against her mother's desires in business but she couldn't remember her mother ever acting so unreasonably.

"I don't see why another company can't provide us the same services," El continued. "I'm not interested in moving forward with them. Let's find another firm."

"We've conferred with several and if you remember, they had the best recommendations by far. I personally know several business owners who have implemented their recommendations and all swore they were the best. We need to hire this firm."

"I'm done talking about this, dear," El said calmly, looking Chloe straight in the eye. It was a nonverbal "stand down" glare.

"Ma! This doesn't make sense." Chloe was becoming visibly agitated. "We need to do what's best for the company and letting these women walk out that door without agreeing to the plan they've laid out will not be a good business decision."

El cast her eyes upward. "You'll never understand. I'll be in my office." El left Chloe where she was standing.

Chloe held her head in her hands and gathered herself before heading back into the room with the consultants. She was so angry and embarrassed she could literally cry, but she couldn't let them see her that way.

They were a bridge she didn't want to burn. Mar-Comm's services didn't come cheap, but their work and results were often stellar. If Chandlers wanted to become the sought-after venue amongst their newly desired audience, they were the firm to take them to the next level. With their fresh ideas and proven track record in building brands with younger audiences, signing on with them was the thing to do.

Chloe didn't go against El's wishes often, but El also had never made bad business decisions rashly either. Her mother was an astute businesswoman. Today, her emotions were getting in the way. Their company couldn't afford that and Chloe refused to see it suffer. As long as they achieved their desired results, she was sure El would get over the fact that Chloe went against her judgment.

After a deep breath, Chloe joined Kathy and Lynne in the conference room. "Sorry about that, ladies." She took her seat. "Now where were we?"

Kathy and Lynne exchanged questionable glances again. Lynne reiterated the end of their presentation before El walked out.

"I appreciate the work you put into this proposal and I love your ideas. I truly think this is what we need to accomplish our goals and take Chandler to the next level. Now if you could offer insight on the media plan you've put together that would be great. I'm excited and look forward to getting started."

Kathy and Lynne looked at each other again. This time, they smiled. Lynne took the reins and outlined their plans for raising Chandler's profile in the media. When Lynne finished reviewing the proposed campaign, Chloe stood and shook their hands.

"Thank you. We'll have our attorneys review the contract and get a signed copy over to you within the week."

"Wonderful! We are really looking forward to working with you."

Chloe nodded. "Me, too. I'll walk you out."

Chloe engaged them in small talk as she accompanied them to the door. She knew she'd have to deal with El for making this decision. Once she saw the results, she was sure that El would get over her issues with the firm she was hiring.

Chapter 10

Donovan spent the better part of his morning sifting through emails before shifting gears to refining budgets for both sides of the family business. His mother ran the catering business and his father ran their real-estate development enterprises. Rivers Development Group built and managed luxury state-of-the-art residences, mostly in urban settings as well as a few office parks across Long Island. Donovan's father had acquired La Belle Riviere for a steal from the previous owner when the real-estate marketing bubble burst. Mrs. Rivers took extreme pleasure in spearheading the renovation and turning it into the stunning venue it was today.

Donovan ran his hands down his face and cupped his yawn. Late-night phone conversations with Chloe were getting the best of him. He chuckled at the memory. He hadn't spent that much time on the phone with a woman, or girl for that matter, since he was a teenager. Donovan enjoyed their talks, which ranged from reminiscing about their time in Puerto Rico to serving as sounding boards for issues and ideas around their careers. He had become attracted to Chloe's mind.

Donovan knew it was more than just a busy schedule that kept Chloe from spending time with him in person. It was time to change that.

"Donovan, darling!" Joliet Rivers's tall slim figure appeared in the doorway, steering him from his thoughts of Chloe. She leaned against the doorframe in a sharp black-and-white suit, red designer pumps and a chic bun at the base of her neck. Crimson lips set a stark contrast against her fair skin. Joliet loved red and would always find a way to incorporate it into any look. "Come for dinner tonight, dear! We're having company and there's someone I'd like you to meet." It was a directive, not an invitation. Invitations could be declined.

"Is this business or personal, Mom?" Donovan sat back. He wondered if this would be another attempt to hook him up with someone's daughter, niece, neighbor, etc.

Instead of responding, she smiled dubiously. "Dinner will be ready at seven." She raised one brow. "Please don't be late, sweetie." Joliet sauntered away from Donovan's door, leaving behind her signature scent, a lily-based perfume that his father adored.

Donovan smiled and shook his head, but he already knew he wouldn't be interested. Mrs. Rivers's meddling was well intentioned but it never turned out well for Donovan. A beautiful face and gorgeous body was just the beginning. What stimulated him the most was a woman that could kindle his mind with titillating conversation. He had that with Chloe.

One thing he learned about Chloe through their extensive discussions was that she was fiercely loyal and he believed that was what kept her from moving beyond great conversation with him.

Spending time with her in Puerto Rico had been like an appetizer for Donovan. He wanted a more substantial helping of time with Chloe now that his appetite had been so deliciously whetted. He smiled at the thought of the plans that he'd set in motion for the coming weekend. He just had to convince Chloe to actually go.

Donovan picked up his cell phone and tapped out a

text to his contact for Friday evening. They responded by texting, We're all set. See you Friday. Donovan sat back feeling accomplished. He only wished Friday would come sooner.

Donovan took a conference call with his business partners about the property they were investing in and attended a business meeting on behalf of his father since Mr. Rivers had to spend his day in their Manhattan office.

By the time he reached his home, one of the few highrise luxury condominiums on Long Island, he was mentally and physically drained. A quick shower refreshed him only slightly before he headed over to his parents' sprawling estate along the North Shore.

"You look quite dapper, sweetie." Joliet kissed his cheek and patted his arm when he walked into the house. "We're still waiting on a few people. If you're hungry, grab some canapés from the kitchen. I'll be right back, okay?" Joliet strolled off before Donovan could respond.

"You look great, too, Mom." Donovan credited his mom for being classy and stylish. She'd shed her polished business attire and replaced it with a flowing floral halter dress that swept the floor as she strode. Her lipstick was the same vibrant red as the flowers in her dress.

"Thank you, Donnie." She smiled appreciatively.

Joliet's lengthy legs gracefully carried her up one side of their winding staircase. When she reached the upper landing, she looked down at Donovan and smiled before disappearing into her master bedroom. It was then that Donovan realized the soft music floating through the home's intercom speakers. The sound of his brother and father's laughter met the music and flowed through the first floor. His father's deep timbre bellowed from the kitchen. He headed there.

"Hey!" William Rivers opened his arms and Donovan

stepped toward him. William patted his back with strong, large hands.

"What's up, Dad?" He turned toward his brother, holding a glass of red wine. "Dayton." He nodded a greeting in his direction before they lightly bumped shoulders. Dayton handed him the glass of wine he had just poured.

"Mrs. Saxton," Donovan sang. "How's my favorite lady?"

Grace Saxton pursed her thin lips and placed her hands on her hips. "Don't let your mother hear you say that." She giggled and pulled Donovan into her embrace. Tilting back, she studied his face endearingly. "Are you hungry?"

"I'm always for your cooking!" Donovan said matter-of-factly.

Grace swatted his arm lightly. "You boys sure know how to make an old lady feel good." She walked over to one of the expertly decorated platters full of strategically lined canapés. "Here." She picked one up and lifted it toward Donovan's mouth. "Taste this." She stood back, head up, sporting a confident grin.

Donovan bit down and rolled his eyes upward. "That's delicious, Mrs. Saxton."

She smiled, obviously happy to meet Donovan's approval. Her plump cheeks reddened slightly.

Donovan shook his head. "Absolutely delicious," he said, covering his full mouth.

Donovan took a seat at the table with his father and brother. Grace placed a sample plate in front of him with an array of different canapés. She was more like an aunt than a housekeeper. She'd been part of his family for as long as he could remember.

Just as he joined his father and brother's lively conversation about who beat who on the golf course a few weeks back, the doorbell rang.

Grace looked toward the foyer, leaning her ear in that

direction. She laid the spoon down on a porcelain rest, wiped her hands in a dishtowel and headed for the door. "I'm getting it, Mrs. Rivers."

"Thanks, Grace," Joliet called from upstairs.

Donovan heard the rustle of several people entering the vast home. Grace led them to the sitting room and promised to return with drinks.

"So who are our guests tonight?" Donovan turned and asked his father.

"Yes, Dad. Mom made it seem like tonight's dinner was pretty important," Dayton added.

"Oh," Donovan said when the realization hit him. "So you have no clue what's happening either."

"Mom 'invited' me this afternoon. Only her words sounded more like a directive than an invitation." Dayton smirked and Donovan shot him a knowing look.

"Yes. Those invitations…" their father said.

Grace returned with a tray of her decadent peach tea, topped with juicy slices of plump organic peaches before leaving again.

"Let's greet our guests," Mr. Rivers stated, standing erect to his full six feet and three inches. He had always taken good care of himself and had been quite the athlete in his youth. Even now he managed to maintain his build. The salt-and-pepper hair framing his smooth skin seemed premature. Gray hair usually made people look older, but against William's face, it simply seemed energetic and appealing. He and Joliet appeared as perfect as Barbie and Ken.

Donovan and Dayton stood with Mr. Rivers and together the trio strolled into the sitting room to greet their guests.

Mr. Rivers led the introductions. It was obvious to Donovan that his father wasn't any more familiar with their visitors than they were. Immediately he noticed the two stunning women that accompanied the older short woman with the big presence and the much taller gentleman that stood protectively by her side. Donovan and Dayton passed quick knowing looks. Their silent but clear dialogue confirmed that this was a setup. The two gorgeous women were an obvious indication.

"Joli will be down momentarily," Mr. Rivers assured them after exchanging pleasantries. "I understand you're a golfer." He directed his inquiry to Roland Creighton—the husband.

"I am. You?" Roland confirmed and asked.

"For sure."

A bright smile eased across Mr. Rivers's face. Donovan knew then that golf would dominate the better part of their conversation during the evening.

"Hello!" Joliet sang as she entered the room like a cool, welcome breeze. Obviously more familiar with their guests than everyone else. "Tiffany, you look absolutely gorgeous," she said, scanning the woman before hugging her.

"Thank you, Joliet. Your dress is fabulous."

As if on cue, Grace entered with a tray of canapés and set them on the coffee table before smiling pleasantly and disappearing as quickly as she'd entered.

"I see your girls have met our boys." Joliet smiled. "They're beautiful." Tilting her head, she grinned at Donovan and winked.

"Savannah. Serita. Come meet Mrs. Joliet Rivers." The twins flanked their mother, towering over her on each side. "We met at the membership meeting for the women's organization I joined a few weeks back. We hit it off right away and vowed to do dinner soon after and now here we are."

"It's a pleasure to meet you, Mrs. Rivers." They shook her hand, one after the other.

"Serita works in commercial banking and Savannah will be entering medical school in the fall."

"Welcome to New York, ladies. I hope you enjoy living here on Long Island. It's a great place to live."

"Thank you," Serita said. Savannah smiled in agreement.

"I'm sure my boys will be happy to show you around." She looked over at Donovan and Dayton and stretched her eyes.

Grace entered the room again. Delicately clapped her hands together, lifted her chin and smiled. "Dinner is served," she announced.

Joliet led the way to the dining room. William took his usual seat, which was opposite Joliet at the large round table that was large enough to seat twelve. Joliet had Grace remove four of the chairs to make the seating for eight appear a little more intimate. She didn't like seeing empty chairs.

After a quick grace from the man of the house, they began to indulge in the small feast Grace had prepared. The group sat before a vibrant arrangement of *niçoise* salad. The center of the table boasted elegantly plated wild-caught king salmon, mouthwatering slices of chateaubriand, champagne risotto, roasted eggplant, peppers and asparagus and sweet summer corn.

Tiffany raved about the delicious spread as they dined and talked more about how she and Joliet met and seemed to have become fast friends. Tiffany expressed her desire to become familiar with her new city, which served as the catalyst for her joining the organization. She and Roland had relocated from Chicago for him to take on his new role as CEO of a top investment firm headquartered along the border of Nassau and Suffolk. The girls would also begin new careers right there on Long Island.

After dinner, Grace offered their company a choice of fresh organic strawberries topped with her homemade whipped cream or her decadent chocolate coconut cake.

After dessert, the parents returned to one of their sitting rooms for cocktails while the twins, Dayton and Donovan headed out back to the gazebo.

"We're so sorry," Serita, the oldest of the twins by a minute and a half, said just after they sat comfortably.

"For what?" Dayton asked.

"Our parents—specifically our mother," Savannah continued for her sister. "They mean well, I'm sure."

"In that case, we'll need to apologize for our parents as well—specifically our mother," Donovan said. The four laughed. "She's always playing the matchmaker."

"We didn't want to be rude," Serita said. "But we felt it was important to let you know that we're both in serious relationships. Our boyfriends are back in Chicago, but we have no intentions of breaking up."

"We totally understand." Donovan held his hand up as if he were surrendering.

"We certainly wouldn't mind being friends. It would be great to have some guidance with becoming familiar with New York," Savannah said.

"Then I'm your man," Dayton volunteered. "I'll tell you all you need to know and if you need a ride, I've got you covered there, too. Friends?" Dayton extended his hand. They all shook as if sealing an agreement.

Donovan felt instant relief. As pretty as these girls were, he hadn't been interested and wondered how he might have to let one of them down. He wanted to give this thing with Chloe a chance.

"Great!" Serita almost squealed. "Our boyfriends will be visiting next weekend so it would be helpful if you could suggest some nice restaurants and a few interesting places we could go in the city."

"You got it," Dayton said. "Take my number." The four of them exchanged numbers.

Now that the pressure had been removed from the atmosphere, they felt free to enjoy themselves. The conversation lightened and getting to know each other became interesting. As cool as the twins seemed, Donovan couldn't help but notice that conversation with them wasn't as intriguing as his chats with Chloe.

When the Creightons left, Dayton and Donovan helped Grace clean up. William retreated to his favorite chair in the family room and Joliet changed into a comfortable caftan.

"So what do you think of the girls? They were stunning, weren't they?" Joliet's eyes sparkled as she entered the kitchen, leaned against the counter and bit into a bright red strawberry.

Donovan and Dayton looked at each other.

"Yes. They were stunning…" Donovan started.

"And taken," Dayton continued.

"Stunningly taken," Donovan concluded, snickering at his mother's chiding glare. She tried to hide her smile but couldn't once they started laughing. Even Grace's shoulders shook from trying to contain her laugh from the opposite side of the room.

"Nice try, Mom." Donovan kissed her cheek. "But I'll find my own lady, thank you."

"When?" She threw her hands up and let them fall at her side.

"It may be sooner than you think," Donovan teased.

Joliet narrowed her eyes at him and tossed the same glare in Dayton's direction, which made them laugh even harder.

Joliet sighed. "I have some other friends with beautiful daughters that you could meet."

"You have more friends with daughters?" Dayton asked incredulously. "Because I could have sworn we'd met them all."

Joliet's mouth opened and closed once she realized they were messing with her.

"You boys!" She pursed her lips and put her hands on her hips.

"We love you, Mom, but we really don't need your help," Donovan said carefully. He didn't want to hurt their mother's feelings.

"We know you mean well, but our idea of the ideal woman is apparently different than what you think." Dayton shrugged matter-of-factly.

"So what is the ideal woman?" Joliet seemed exasperated.

"No. No. No." Donovan wagged his finger. "We're not going there." He kissed his mother again. "I'll see you in the morning. Good night." He turned before she could say anything else.

Dayton followed suit and headed behind Donovan, leaving Joliet in the kitchen to wonder.

The moment he got in his car, he dialed Chloe's number. Something about meeting those twins made his desire to move forward with Chloe stronger.

"Hey, you!" Her soft voice filled the line, sounding a little deeper than usual.

"Did I wake you?" he asked.

"No. I was lying down, but I wasn't asleep."

"Because you were waiting for my call, right?"

Chloe's chuckle was like a soft breeze blowing in his ear.

"Sure. Yeah. Right." She laughed louder.

After delighting in the sound of her laughter, Donovan's words flew from his brain and ran straight past his lips. "We're going out Friday…" He paused, giving her a moment to object as he knew she would. Before she could fumble through the start of her protest, Donovan cut her off. "And I refuse to take no for an answer."

Chapter 11

Chloe absolutely loved the ideas that the women from MarComm proposed. She was even more confident about her decision to override her mother's opposition and hire their firm. They were still in the process of finalizing their agreement but Chloe wouldn't wait to move forward on their idea to host a sampling reception. They would invite businesses and individuals on a potential list of targeted clients. This event would offer prospective customers an opportunity to tour their venue, sample foods from their unique menu and view a presentation communicating why Chandlers would be the ideal location for their next event.

Timing was critical. They often received many requests to book events during the months of May, June and July. Chloe wanted to take advantage of this high season and hold the event before the end of June. She'd been working on El but her mother was stubborn. She knew that El liked the ideas the consultants presented but she refused to acknowledge them. El was still pretty angry with Chloe for moving forward with negotiations against her orders. El gave Chloe the cold shoulder for days until Bobby Dale finally intervened.

Chloe navigated the catering hall with a cheerful bounce. However, as excited as she was, it was hard to keep her focus on all the great things happening at Chandlers. Chloe's mind kept shifting to Donovan's refusal to accept no for an answer. It wasn't that she didn't want to go out with him. She just didn't think it made much sense to date someone who she could never enjoy a long-term relationship with. Their families would never get along. She could only imagine how El would act.

It was unfortunate. Donovan seemed like a long-term kind of guy. Chloe felt so comfortable talking to him and remembered how easily she was able to relax in his presence by the time they left Puerto Rico. Donovan made her laugh, think and even challenge herself both personally and professionally. They swapped silly childhood stories and reveled in how much they had in common. Under different circumstances, Donovan would be the perfect guy for Chloe.

Chloe looked at the time in the lower right corner of her laptop and sighed. The end of the day was almost here and she still hadn't thought of a way to let Donovan down easily. So far, she'd been unsuccessful in convincing him that going out may not be in their best interest. She loved their discussions but didn't want to mislead him. There was no way they could take things any further.

It wasn't about defying her mother, though she was fiercely loyal to her. Chloe never liked conflict and didn't want to deal with the drama of bad blood messing up their family relationships. She thought about calling Jewel. She'd yet to tell her that Donovan planned to take her out later. She already knew what Jewel would say: "Go" and "No one has to know."

Chloe rested her head against the back of her chair. Closing her eyes, she remembered how much fun they'd had at karaoke night. How awed Donovan was when he'd heard her sing. Quick flashes of the time they spent together played in her mind's eye as if she was flipping through a picture book. She saw the balcony in the restaurant; moonlight rippling on the navy blue sea, the caverns and the night they had sailed. She felt his lips on hers.

Chloe's breath caught. Her head snapped up, eyes popped open and her hand flew to her heart. She looked around even though she was in her office alone.

Chloe didn't want to be done with Donovan. She decided to go. Jewel was right. No one had to know. She breezed through the remainder of her day with a depth of excitement.

Two minutes after five o'clock found Chloe in her car. She escaped the office before El could come asking what she had planned for the evening. She didn't want to lie to her mother but couldn't possibly tell the truth.

By seven thirty, Chloe had a light snack, showered and dressed in an electric blue, strapless jumpsuit. She ran the flat iron through her hair, eliminating the bit of frizz that the humid day generated. When the doorbell rang, Chloe's stomach released a swarm of butterflies. She stood still and gathered herself before heading for the door.

Chloe's cell phone rang. She continued to the door, letting Donovan in before excusing herself and retreating quickly to retrieve her cell phone. It was El. Chloe was glad to have missed her mother's call. She dropped her phone into her evening purse and went back to greet her company.

Chloe could see Donovan's appreciation for the effort she put into preparing for her date. She couldn't help her demure smile.

"You look great," Donovan said with a sigh. He kissed her cheek.

"Thanks." She looked him over without shame. "You look pretty good yourself."

"Are you ready for another adventure?" Donovan asked. His voice dipped slightly lower.

Chloe shrugged her shoulder and raised her brows. "I guess so." Donovan's lips spread into an easy smile. Chloe suddenly felt aware of her femininity and that flirtatious spark she had sensed in Puerto Rico returned. Tilting her head slightly, she locked eyes with him. Everything else in the room seemed to disappear. "I'm ready." Chloe snickered, realizing how her comment could have easily been taken out of context. Her voice sounded husky and she blushed, yet let the possible double entendre hang in her air.

Donovan cleared his throat and his smile broadened. "We'd better get going." Opening the door, he stepped back to allow her to walk out first.

When Chloe stepped past Donovan, she felt a jolt of electricity rush through her. She stood rigidly to avoid shuddering in front of him. Chloe swallowed and continued through the door.

Donovan opened the car door for Chloe before rounding the back of the car to the driver's side. Inside, he set the radio to a jazz station.

"How many excuses did you think about telling me before you finally decided to go out with me?"

Chloe's telltale smile hid behind tucked-in lips. "What makes you think I came up with excuses?" Donovan looked at her sideways as if her question was ridiculous. Chloe replied with laughter.

"This won't be the last date either, you hear me?" Donovan proclaimed.

"Wow! You're bossy." Chloe shook her head, flattered by the notion that Donovan wanted to continue seeing her. His smile was like a shot of whiskey—intoxicating and causing her heart to spread in her chest. She felt giddy. Donovan had a way of making her feel like a schoolgirl with a crush. In his presence, Chloe became hyperaware of her femininity. Playful banter accompanied them all the way to Manhattan.

Donovan pulled into a parking space as another car was

pulling out. "Perfect timing," he said, maneuvering the car into an impeccable parallel park.

They exited the car near Washington Square Park. The downtown streets were filled as they usually were on a Friday night. Taking Chloe by the hand, Donovan led her through the crowd.

After two short blocks, he steered her down a short flight of stairs into a trendy lounge. Blue lights lined the underside of the bar top. Fancy liquor bottles lined glass shelves in front of a water feature. A live band played a popular R & B soul song on a small stage. The lead singer's raspy voice floated through the small space, creating a sultry vibe. She reminded Chloe of the singer Jill Scott. She, too, had a pretty face and curvy frame. Her voice was potent enough to reach inside of you and plug right into your emotions.

Chloe bobbed her head to the music. Almost every table was occupied. The hostess guided them to a spot right up front. Chloe looked around, taking in the mellow atmosphere as they took their seats. Instantly, she fell in love with the place and imagined being the one onstage.

Donovan excused himself to go to the restroom. Chloe's smile was instinctive. The singer's voice seemed to flow right through her. It had been so long since Chloe had been in a place like this. She wondered why and promised herself that she'd get out more often.

Donovan returned, leaned in and asked if she was enjoying herself.

"I'm having an amazing time already."

"Great!"

A waiter came by and they ordered drinks and a meal, which turned out to be absolutely delicious. She sipped her cocktail as the singer took to the stage after a short break. Chloe looked forward to hearing her sing again.

She looked over at Donovan and caught him staring at her again. She smiled.

They didn't talk much inside the lounge but their nonverbal communication was companionable. Donovan held her hand and they tapped their fingers to the rhythms that overtook the entire room.

Suddenly Donovan stood. "Can I have this dance?"

"Sure." Chloe stood and stepped into his arms and they swayed to the music. She was limber in Donovan's arms. No tension existed there. They danced for a few songs and returned to their seats.

"Still having a good time?" Donovan leaned closely and asked.

"I'm having a great time. Thank you for making me get out tonight."

"I have a surprise for you and I hope you like it." Donovan sipped his cocktail.

Chloe's smile spread across her face. "I love surprises." Donovan's magnified smile made her feel as if she'd made his day.

They sipped some more and when the singer called her name, Chloe looked around as if she were referring to another Chloe.

"Ms. Chloe, will you do us the honor of joining us onstage tonight?" the woman said into the microphone.

Chloe's eyes widened and she set them on Donovan. He pointed to the stage. "Seems they're paging you. You'd better go." A conspicuous smile played at the corner of his lips.

"Donovan! You didn't!"

"Come on, Ms. Chloe," the Jill Scott look-a-like coaxed. "Y'all help me welcome her." The crowd burst into applause.

"Yeah, Ms. Chloe," one patron yelled.

"Are you going to sing for us, Ms. Chloe?" another shouted.

"Your audience awaits." Donovan stood and held his hand out to her.

Slowly, Chloe stood and took his hand. Applause erupted again. Donovan guided her to the stage as one would a queen to her throne.

Chloe climbed the two steps, mounting the stage. She looked over the room. People were still applauding, calling out her name. It all felt surreal.

"Yes! Let's give Ms. Chloe a hand." The singer clapped with the microphone in one hand. "What would you like to sing for us tonight?"

Chloe thought for a moment. Instead of coming up with a song, she was taken aback. It was like déjà vu. Chloe remembered being a young girl and imagining herself standing before adoring crowds. A mix of fear and exhilaration filled her lungs. She took a deep breath.

"What song?" she repeated to herself, forcing her mind to return to the present. Donovan had returned to his seat. She looked down at him and he gave her a reassuring nod.

As she stared into his smiling face, a song came to her. She told the singer, who shared her selection and cued the band before handing Chloe the microphone. She'd chosen a classic by an old-school R & B soul artist that her mother loved to listen to and she loved to sing.

"Ladies and gentlemen, Ms. Chloe Chandler!" The woman led another round of applause.

Chloe lifted the microphone to her mouth. Once again, she looked over the audience, now seeing them as a group of individuals instead of one blurry boisterous cluster. She looked into the faces of several people. They encouraged her with a nod or smile. Some of them shouted out to her again.

"You can do it."

"Don't be shy, honey."

"She looks like she can sing." She could tell by the timbre of the voice that this statement was made by an older woman.

Chloe looked back at the band. The drummer lifted his head. Chloe nodded hers and he began playing the song she'd given to the singer. The pianist joined in next, followed by the guitarist, until each musician added his or her own flow.

Chloe closed her eyes one last time, opened her mouth and started singing. Immediately, she felt at peace. The rhythm seeped inside of her, compelling Chloe to move to the melody. At first, the crowd quieted. Chloe was aware of the intense silence but kept singing. She could hear the rumble of the crowd grow louder.

Chloe matched the original artist riff for riff, perfectly laying her beautiful voice over the notes. She reached the bridge and belted out the lyrics with everything inside of her. By the time she opened her eyes, her skin was moist from sweat. Every person in the lounge was on their feet, clapping, shouting her name, whistling.

Chloe felt like crying at the sight of it all. Her heart was filled with gratitude. She would always remember feeling this euphoric.

Chloe searched for Donovan. She spotted him. He beamed with pride. She took a bow and handed the microphone back. The applause continued as she returned to her table. She fell into Donovan's arms. At first, he embraced her. After a moment, he pulled away from, held her face in his hands and covered her lips with his. Donovan kissed her as if he'd never let go. Chloe knew then that she'd never forget this night.

Chapter 12

Donovan didn't want to let Chloe go. His chest instinctively puffed when she'd come off the stage and walked right into his arms. Before he realized what he'd done, Donovan had pulled her face to his and lost himself in their kiss. He was brought back to reality by the whooping of the crowd cheering on their affectionate display.

"Now that's how you let someone know they did a great job," the lead singer said in jest and laughter filled the small lounge.

Chloe ended the kiss with a peck, squeezed her eyes shut and giggled toward the floor. They had everyone's attention and Donovan could tell she was slightly embarrassed.

"I couldn't help myself. You were amazing." Donovan embraced her one more time before pulling out her chair for her to sit.

Chloe's smile was endless. "How did you manage that?"

"What?"

"Getting them to let me sing?"

"I'm very persuasive and usually get what I want." Donovan left it there.

"Really, Donovan." Chloe's expression told him she wasn't buying his answer.

"Okay. An old friend owns the club and I told him I was going to bring you here tonight."

"Very cool!"

The band began to play again. The singer joined in after a musician's jazzy intro. Her voice was beautiful but not like Chloe's.

Chloe's voice ignited something inside of him when she sang. Her perfect pitch left him mesmerized. Awed by her transformation onstage, he watched Chloe intently as she sat across from him, bobbing to the band's rhythm.

Taking her hand in his, Donovan reminisced about the moments before. He saw her back onstage, eyes closed, swaying to the beat, moving her head with the notes. Donovan remembered the way she tapped the beat out on her hip to keep her time. He wanted to join her onstage, wrap his arms around her and dance until the song ended. By the time she'd hit her last note, Donovan desired her even more.

They sat nibbling on appetizers from the limited menu and sipping cocktails through the last set. When the band said their goodbyes, Donovan and Chloe left. Donovan wasn't ready to go home. He took Chloe's hand and they strolled through Washington Square Park.

"That felt so good." Chloe shook her head.

"Would you do it again?"

Chloe inhaled, letting her eyes roll back. She released a sharp breath and shook her vigorously. "Yes. It was euphoric!"

"Good, because a voice like yours is meant to be shared. You shouldn't keep it under wraps."

Chloe shrugged. "I guess." She sighed. "I've been so caught up in work that I put singing aside and forgot how much I enjoyed it."

"You ever thought about pursuing a career in music?"

"Oh Lord, no! That's not my thing. I'm not willing to give up my privacy." Chloe looked down and watched her feet as they walked. "Truthfully, my parents, specifically my mother, would have a conniption fit. She never wanted us to be deluded by dreams where other people were in control of how far you could go. Plus we have our family business."

"You can sing and still run the business."

"It seems like a waste of time." Chloe didn't look convinced about her own statement. She squeezed her shoulders into a dismissive shrug.

"A waste of time to who? You or your family?" Donovan stopped walking and faced her.

Chloe didn't look directly at him. "I'm not so sure."

"At least you're honest." Donovan took her hand and started walking again. "You enjoyed being onstage, didn't you?" he asked.

Chloe's eyes twinkled, even in the moonlight. Wearing a faraway look, she shook her head slowly and her brows knitted as if she were trying to find words. "It was like…" She paused. "A dream! The lights. The people. The standing ovation!" Chloe threw her head back and laughed— the joyful sound reached inside of Donovan and teased his sense of desire once again. "It was incredible."

"My mother loves Anita Baker. What made you choose that song?"

Donovan thought he saw Chloe blush. "Just an old favorite." Chloe kicked a pebble. "My mom used to play her songs all the time. One year she surprised my dad and sang it to him for his birthday. I think my dad cried. He denies it to this day." Chloe chuckled. "I've loved the song ever since. My mother has a beautiful voice, too," Chloe said matter-of-factly.

"I was wondering who you might have gotten that talent from."

"Yes. I haven't heard her sing in years."

"Have you ever sung together?" Donovan asked.

Chloe stopped and bit her bottom lip pensively. "Not since I was a kid."

"Maybe you should one day," Donovan said.

"We will see if that ever happens," Chloe said sarcastically.

After a few more minutes of sauntering through the park, Donovan led Chloe back to the car. He opened her door, waited for her to climb in and gently pushed it shut. Rounding the car, he thought about how to end the night. Donovan wasn't ready to drop her at home. He really wanted to feel her lips again.

When Donovan pulled in front of her home, he shut the engine off and sat back. They sat in silence for a few moments before Donovan took her by the hand.

"Where do you want to go next?"

Chloe huffed and dropped her head. He felt a pause in his chest and wondered if it was his heart. Had she affected him so much already?

"Donovan," Chloe began.

Donovan held his hands up, stopping her impending objection. "I want to see you again and again and again. I want to ride this roller coaster until it flies off the track. I have a good time with you and I want that to continue. I'm not asking you to the altar. Let's enjoy ourselves. It will be our thing."

Chloe's mouth opened but nothing came out. She blew out a breath.

"If you can honestly say you don't enjoy talking it up and spending time with me, we can end this here and now."

Chloe pursed her lips while Donovan held his breath. He'd given her an out but hoped she wouldn't take it. It had never been so important for him to spend time with a woman before.

"Let's have some fun." Chloe tossed her hands up.

Donovan reached over, gently turned her cheek toward

him and kissed her lips again. She tasted somewhat salty. Her soft lips felt good against his. His tongue darted in and out of her mouth and he leaned as close as he could with the console between them. When he released her, they both sat back panting.

"Wanna come in?" Chloe's voice was almost a whisper.

Donovan was out of the car in an instant. He rounded the vehicle, opened the passenger side door and held out his hand. Chloe took it and stepped out of the car. Donovan locked in on her long legs and bit back a grunt. He planned to be a gentleman until she gave him permission to engage further. He would follow Chloe's lead no matter how long it took for her to open up to him intimately.

Chloe took the lead on the walkway up to her door. Donovan followed close behind. Inside, Chloe turned on music and poured two glasses of wine. Donovan didn't pay attention to the tunes or the TV. His focus was squarely on Chloe.

They sat in her den, sipping over light conversation. Donovan watched her lips intently as she spoke. They shifted in and out of easy silence as smoothly as a car changing lanes on an open highway.

After Chloe's second glass of wine, she giggled more. Her motions grew more fluid and girlishness seeping from her, making her more desirable in Donovan's eyes. He treasured the way her chin lifted and her shoulder dipped when she laughed. She seemed carefree. His gut clenched at the playful way she regarded him and blushed from his comments.

Chloe laughed and Donovan covered her mouth, swallowing her laughter. Instantly, their hands roamed one another as if they sought each other through the dark with an eager anticipation for this moment. Just as quickly they lost breath, they caught it again and continued their passionate lock. Donovan drew closer to Chloe. She wrapped her arms around his neck. Chloe leaned back and he lay over her, caressing her perfect C cups through her jumpsuit.

Deep moans and hisses pushed the droning of the radio further into the background. Donovan suddenly became aware of how much Chloe affected him when his manhood pressed against her navel. He ended the kiss with a few endearing pecks and lifted himself off her. He didn't want his body's response to offend her.

Sitting next to Chloe, he looked at her swollen lips. She touched them—intuitively it seemed. He licked his. It was a natural reaction. Looking at her lips created a special kind of hunger.

Chloe's coy smile and the glint in her eye indicated that she knew why he'd pulled away. She glanced down at the bulge in his pants and looked back up at him.

Donovan played with her hair. "I think it's time for me to go." He hoped she would object.

Instead, she breathed deep and let it out slowly but didn't respond. Donovan knew she wanted him as much as he wanted her. Her pebbled nipples and engorged lips told him so. He'd wait until the time was right.

Two slow sensual kisses served as his acknowledgment that it was time to end the night. Donovan stood reluctantly. Chloe followed suit. He needed one more kiss. Locking her fingers between his, he leaned in for another kiss. Her waiting lips received him passionately.

"I better leave right now," he panted when they let one another go.

"I think that's best," she finally agreed.

Chloe walked him to the door—a walk that seemed much farther than when he first arrived. Another peck. It turned into a deeper kiss. They forced themselves apart.

"Sing for me next time," he said close to her lips.

"I will," she whispered.

Donovan became addicted to her voice, needing to hear it daily whether she was singing or not.

Chapter 13

Chloe woke early, feeling giddy from their date. She dressed in shorts and a tank and headed out for an early walk since she hadn't run in months. Her goal was to work her way back up to a good run starting today. Outside, she stopped and held her face to the sky. The warmth felt good on her skin. She was glad to have made it out before the sun burned off the coolness of the night.

Chloe had purchased her home over three years ago but as she made her way along the walking path in her complex, she realized she hadn't paid much attention to how beautiful her neighborhood truly was. She felt as if she was seeing the vibrant roses, lush perennials and perfectly paved winding trail for the first time. She imagined walking the pathway hand-in-hand with Donovan and burst out laughing. She'd never been a sappy, hopeless romantic. What was wrong with her?

After a few laps, Chloe headed back home to prepare for the day ahead—a fulfilling church service and then dinner with the family. Her Aunt Ava Rae was in town and she couldn't wait to see her. Aunt Ava was always ripe with straightforward advice, captivating adventures and outlandish narratives that seemed to defy her astute demeanor. A stunning beauty, she was the aunt all the female cousins wanted to be like and the standard all the male cousins compared their girlfriends to.

Chloe's phone rang as she put her key in the door. Her joy spread throughout her body when she saw Donovan's name across her display.

"You're up early," he said just after her greeting.

"If you weren't expecting me to answer, then why call?" Chloe bit down on the hankering that was burgeoning from the sound of his voice. She wished he were there to kiss her the way he'd done the other night. She wouldn't be able to trust herself around him much longer. He awakened things in her that had been dormant even in her last relationship.

"I was taking a chance. Have you had breakfast?"

"Actually no, but I'm only having a quick bite this morning. I need to get ready for church." She jogged up the stairs to her room.

"What are you doing later?" he asked.

"Dinner with the family. My aunt and uncle are visiting from out of town." Chloe pulled a dress from her walk-in closet, held it up to her torso and looked in the full-length mirror.

"Oh. Okay," he said, sounding disappointed.

Too bad she couldn't invite him to join her for dinner. Her mother's eyes would fly out of her head if she brought Donovan to their home. The thought made her chuckle.

"I won't get to see you today," Donovan said.

"You never know," she teased. Chloe tilted her head, turning side to side with a different dress pressed against her.

"I like the way that sounds. Call me when dinner is over. Maybe we can have a nightcap."

To Chloe, that was code for more heavy petting. If they kept that up, she'd soon burst from all the sexual frustration they were building. She could only imagine what Donovan had had to do to release all that tension and shuddered at the image that appeared in her head.

"Chloe!"

"Huh?" She had zoned him out completely, thinking about his parts. She laid three dresses across the end of her bed trying to decide which to wear to church. She needed something that could easily transition into a comfortable option for dinner with the family.

"Can you hear me?"

"Oh. I can hear you now." Chloe went along as if the cell phone was the reason she'd missed what he'd said. She couldn't admit she'd been thinking about his member. She chose an ivory sheath dress with a blended fabric. It was one of those outfits that could be dressed up or down and appeared to be the coolest option for the hot summer day they were expecting.

"Will Tuesday evening work for you?" Donovan asked.

"Work for what?" She had missed more of the conversation than she'd realized.

"I told you it's a surprise."

"Hold on." Chloe removed the cell phone from her ear, tapped her calendar and checked her availability. "Yes. Tuesday is open. What time?"

"Six thirty?"

"That's fine."

"Good. Call me when you get in later if you feel like talking."

"Sure." Chloe thought his request a little odd since they spoke every night.

"Especially if you feel like having company," Donovan added.

"We'll see about that," Chloe said and laughed already knowing how that could turn out. As much as she wanted to, she wasn't sure if she should go *there* with Donovan.

Chloe ended her call, showered and joined her family at the church they attended since she was a little girl. They headed to her parents' estate after.

Even with amazing cooks, her mother, aunt and grandmother, Mary-Kate, insisted on helping out in the kitchen. In no time, they churned out a delectable spread of roasted veggies, braised meats, fragrant rice, colorful salads and decadent desserts—all variations of Grandma Mary-Kate's recipes.

Chloe's father, Robert Dale, or Bobby Dale as their grandfather said as if it were one word, joined their uncle, grandfather and siblings in the Florida room listening to soul music and chatting.

They sectioned off in groups, Bobby Dale on one side speaking with the older men of the family while the siblings convened at the wicker table. Eventually, they were called in for dinner in the main dining room with a table large enough for the entire family. Grandpa blessed the food and the next sounds were fine china clinking, sweet tea flowing and utensils scraping against plates.

"That sure was good," said their patriarch, Edward Chandler, whom they endearingly called Grandpa Eddie. He was a strapping man with gentle eyes. He sat his burly frame back in the chair.

"Thanks, Grandpa. I made it all by myself." Chloe's youngest sister, Jade, took credit and the table erupted in laughter.

"You wish!" Christian, their only brother, teased, licking his fingers.

"Chris!" El reproved his actions with a glare.

"Sorry, Mom. This dinner is great!" He continued licking his fingers. "You don't see anyone throwing up, do you, Grandpa? That's a clear sign that Jade was nowhere near the kitchen." He continued teasing his sister.

"Hush, Chris. I can cook." Jade squinted her eyes at him.

"You can cook up a hot mess," Chris acknowledged matter-of-factly.

El pursed her lips. "All right now!" she chided even through her laugh.

"I have to admit, all of the women in our family are great cooks," Christian said.

"The men are no slouches," Grandpa Eddie added.

"He's right about that," Bobby Dale agreed. "We don't do it as often but we've got those skills as you young people say," he said, leaning back to allow the housekeepers to pick up his plate.

"Grandma, Grandpa." Jade got their attention. "Does it amaze you that Grandma's pies led to a food empire for the family?"

Grandpa's chest lifted a little and he tossed a proud glance at his wife.

Mary-Kate patted Eddie's knee. "I'm just glad that we were blessed enough to provide for our family. I never expected this when I started making pies for people. The first restaurant was as far as we thought this would go. It was your dad that took things to another level when he got the idea to start Chandler Food Corp." Mary-Kate looked at her son lovingly. "And your mother came up with the idea to open Chandlers. I'm proud of all of you."

"How's business going?" Grandpa asked.

"Well," Bobby Dale chimed in. "We're looking at renovating the kitchen and expanding the warehouse. Jewel's leading that charge, right, honey?"

Smiling proudly, Jewel nodded. "I got some great ideas and met with a few vendors at the convention."

"And over at the restaurant," he said, referring to Chandlers. "El and Chloe are working on some changes to make it a more appealing choice for catering events amongst younger audiences."

"I'll admit. I wasn't too happy when she decided to hire those women from that company that also worked with the Rivers family." El rolled her eyes. "But I must say their ideas have already helped to gain more exposure." El turned to Chloe. "Honey, tell your grandparents about the event."

Chloe felt herself glowing. She trusted that she could take her mother's comment as an indication that her mother was pleased with the work that she was doing even though she never said anything to her directly. "You have to come, Grandma and Grandpa. We're hosting a sampling event that will give businesses and prospective clients an opportunity to experience what it's like to have an event at Chandlers. We've done some renovations to the grounds to spruce things up and revamped the menu. We're already almost at capacity with all the RSVPs we've received."

"That's good news." Grandma Mary-Kate looked pleased.

"I'd say so," Grandpa Eddie said, wiping sweet potato pie from his mouth. "You've got the perfect setting right there on the marina. That view is amazing."

"Absolutely stunning," Mary-Kate added as if Grandpa's choice of words weren't enough.

"What about the foundation?" Grandpa Eddie asked.

Chris cleared his throat. "Going well. We've found a few other organizations we'd like to support," he said, speaking on the part of the Chandler empire that he helped run.

"Good to hear. It wouldn't make sense to gain so much and not put anything back out into the universe. Blessings are meant to be shared," Grandpa Eddie said.

"They sure are." Grandma Mary-Kate nodded in agreement. "The good book says, to whom much is given, much is expected."

"As bright and pretty as you girls are, when are we going to meet some men? And where's your woman, Chris? I'm ready for grandnieces and nephews," Aunt Ava Rae said. "It doesn't look like my boys plan on making me a grandmother anytime soon."

The siblings took turns looking at each other before laughing.

"I'm with her," Grandma Mary-Kate said. "We want to have some great-grandchildren to spoil someday, right, Eddie?"

"Sure do. We need somebody to pass the businesses down to." Grandpa nodded at the elders who all nodded back in agreement.

"It sure would be nice to have some grandkids running around here," Bobby Dale said.

"As long as they find the *right*—" El paused a moment to let that word sink in. She peered at each of her children over her designer glasses "—partners," she continued. "We can't just have anybody joining the family." She didn't seem as enthusiastic as the others.

Chloe wondered what El would say if she knew how much time she'd been spending with Donovan.

"Right now, I'm focusing on building the business," Chloe said.

"Don't forget to have a life in the process," Ava Rae said. "No one on their death bed ever wished they worked more hours."

"That's right," Uncle Benjamin said, cosigning his wife's statement. "Life will pass you right by if you let it."

"Yep," Grandma added.

"When I find the one worthy of bringing home, you'll all know," Jewel said. "I'm not shy," she said with a discreet glance toward Chloe. "I just have standards." Her siblings responded with a mix of head shakes and eye rolls.

"I wonder if there's anyone out there capable of meeting those standards," Chris said under his breath but loudly enough for everyone to hear.

Jewel tossed her cloth napkin at him. "You're talking, playboy?"

Chloe, Jewel and Jade all laughed, knowing how their brother breezed through women, leaving them heartbroken in his wake.

"It's like shopping," Chris began. "You check out your options," he continued, despite the incredulous glares from all three of his sisters. "Try on a few outfits to see what fits well. One day, you'll find the ideal one and bring that home with you. I haven't found that perfect fit yet. Plus, I'm young. I still have time."

"Ha! That's my boy!" Grandpa chuckled.

"Eddie!" Grandma tossed him a sideways glance. She turned to Chris. "Find you a nice girl to settle down with. She better know how to cook."

Everyone laughed.

"I think when I meet her, I'll instinctively know she's the right one, but I'm in no rush," Chris said, swiping his hands from one side to the other punctuating his comment.

"What about that Madison girl?" El asked. "She seemed nice and she comes from a good family." By "good," she meant a family with an impressive pedigree. That mattered to their mother.

Chloe, Jewel and Jade all looked away, knowing what a scandalous mess that Tiffany Madison was. Chris reared back and shook his head. "Too superficial. That's the problem with a lot of these women. I mean, I love a good-looking lady but when I settle down, I want her to care about more than the names she wears and the cars she drives."

"That's true," Ava Rae said. She turned to the sisters. "We'll talk, ladies," she said, pointing her dessert fork. "I'll give you some tips for snagging the good ones." She winked and blew a kiss at her husband, banking tycoon

Benjamin Gainesville. He responded with a smile, staring at her as if he wanted to ravish her right there at the table.

They laughed but Chloe planned to take her up on that offer. It was a known fact that Uncle Benjamin and their four sons doted on his wife as if she were royalty. Even as signs of aging began to settle in her beautiful middle-aged face, she turned the heads of men both young and old. They tripped over themselves to get her attention before realizing she was married. After finding out, some still didn't care. Ava Rae held the key to wooing men without even trying and Chloe wanted to find out what it was. Perhaps she could use those techniques with Donovan.

A slight gasp escaped Chloe's mouth, briefly capturing everyone's attention. She cleared her throat and coughed as if she could have been choking. She held her hand up, waving off any concern from her family. Surprising herself, she couldn't believe that thought that had just passed through her mind.

She shouldn't be concerned about wooing a man that she could never bring home.

Chapter 14

Donovan looked at the clock on the dashboard as he pulled his sports car into his designated garage space. Wondering if Chloe had made it back from her parents', he retrieved his cell phone. He didn't want to go up to his place if she was willing to have company.

"Hello," Chloe answered on the first ring.

Donovan bit his bottom lip. The sound of her voice taunted his senses. "Hey. Did you make it home yet?"

"Yep. I'm sitting on my couch watching the home decorating channel. I get ideas for the restaurant when I watch these shows."

"Would you mind some company for a little while? I'm not ready to go home yet." Donovan held his breath awaiting her answer.

"Sure."

"Be right there." Donovan backed out of his garage and headed to Chloe's. He promised himself he'd control his urges around her.

When he arrived at her place, he popped his trunk and pulled out a choice bottle of wine. Always searching for the best options for their catering hall, he kept bottles handy. It wasn't his first time at her place but he never entered empty-handed. Being that it was Sunday, most stores were already closed for the evening.

Chloe opened the door wearing ripped jeans and a tank

top. Seeing her bare thighs through the pants gave him pause.

"Good evening." Donovan kissed her cheek and presented her with the wine.

"Thanks," Chloe said, taking the bottle from him. She closed and locked the door and headed to the den.

Donovan followed behind. He enjoyed being in her space. It smelled of lavender and vanilla. Chloe invited him to sit in the den before disappearing and returning with two glasses. Donovan popped open the wine and filled each glass halfway. He noticed the television playing. She was still watching design shows.

"You're redecorating Chandlers?" he asked.

"Oh no!" She wagged her fingers. "I'm not giving up any information. You're the competition, remember?" she teased.

"Really?" Donovan gave her a sideways glance.

Chloe threw her head back and laughed. The urge to kiss her exposed neck overwhelmed Donovan for a moment.

"How's the consultant thing going?"

"I really like them. Thanks for the recommendation. You were right. They are the best in business."

"Does your mother know I referred them?" Donovan looked mischievous.

"Of course not! For the record, I chose to work with them because of their reviews and they came with the most thorough presentation and innovative ideas. I met with three other consulting firms before making my final decision."

"Because you're a smart businesswoman." Donovan's finger grazed her chin. He thought he saw her shudder a little. "I'm glad to hear things are going well." He placed his hand in his lap. His finger tingled from touching her face.

"We're working on planning a reception for clients. I would invite you to come, but you know." Chloe giggled.

"Maybe I'd show up."

"You wouldn't!" Chloe laughed. "I couldn't even imagine my mother's face if you walked in there."

"I wouldn't want to imagine it. I'm sure Joliet would respond in a similar way."

"Our parents." Chloe shook her head.

"If they knew we were here together…" Donovan let the thought hang.

Chloe groaned. "They'd die."

When their laughter died down, the atmosphere seemed heavy.

"We laugh, but it's really unfortunate." Donovan's tone was serious.

"How so?" Chloe asked.

At first, Donovan narrowed his gaze, contemplating if he should be completely honest with her. "For us. It's unfortunate for us." Chloe looked down at her nails. Donovan lifted her chin, forcing her to look directly into his eyes. He wanted her to know his words were sincere. "It would be easier to like you so much." Donovan watched her swallow, then clear her throat. "I would have no problem telling my mother about you…if we were to become serious, that is. I know it would be hard for you."

Chloe sighed, averting her eyes once again. "I kind of like it like this," Chloe said, then cracked a mischievous smile, letting on that she was teasing. "I feel so rebellious and I like it."

That made Donovan chuckle even though he was serious. There was so much to like about Chloe, she was easy to talk to, smart, talented and beautiful—the full package. Their conversations flowed effortlessly from one subject to another, covering everything from work to sports and goals.

Before Chloe, he couldn't remember talking to any woman as much. They often did other things to fill their time together. As much as he wanted Chloe, their dialogue was as intriguing as their heavy petting.

Speaking of which, Donovan's sight settled on her lips. She wore a pale pink gloss this evening. Her plump lips held a sparkling sheen.

"We can't always control what we feel," Donovan added.

"I know." Chloe's expression grew serious. She shifted her position on the couch, sitting rigidly.

"What if it happened with us?"

Chloe pressed her lips together. "I don't know."

Donovan wasn't concerned about his family in the same way Chloe was about hers. He wasn't concerned about how anyone felt when it came to the people he cared about. However, he understood and respected Chloe's apprehension. He knew she was her own woman but the idea of upsetting the family troubled her. He wished it didn't.

"They'd accept whomever I chose to date," he said, speaking of his family.

"My mother is different." That's all she said.

Donovan accomplished his goal. He didn't want to pressure her too much but he wanted her to at least consider the possibilities. He didn't plan to be her scandalous little secret for too much longer.

Chloe looked contrite. He needed to release the tension in the room.

"Oh!" He stood. "I need to get something out of the car."

"What is it?" Chloe called to his back.

"Give me a second." Donovan was out the door and returned moments later with a chessboard in his hand.

"Ah! You up for a challenge?"

Chloe covered her mouth and laughed. "Always."

"Get ready to lose. I'm not the type to let pretty girls

win just because." Donovan set the chessboard on the table and dragged it closer to their couch where they sat.

Chloe curled her feet up on the couch and positioned herself comfortably it seemed. "I might be pretty but I don't lose easily."

Donovan clapped his hands together and rubbed them. "We'll see." He set up the board. "I'll even let you go first."

"Get ready for the smackdown!" Chloe announced, taking a sip of her wine.

"I talk a lot of mess when I play so don't get scared," Donovan teased.

"You can't distract me with that crap. You had better focus on your game. I don't waste time conquering opponents."

"Your trash-talking game is almost as good as mine." His wisecrack compliment tickled her.

After his first loss, Donovan was in awe. Her second win bruised his ego.

"Who's the master?" Chloe gloated. She stood, swung her hands over her head while gyrating her hips in a victory dance.

What Donovan should have seen as silly, he deemed sexy. Heat bolted through his gut and settled in his groin. He watched her with a smile, loving how this refined woman let loose.

"One more game?" Chloe sat down and reached for the board.

Donovan put her hand over his. She released the knight she was holding. Donovan was sure she'd felt that flash of electricity pass between them.

"I'm done playing with you." He meant that in several ways.

Chloe looked at him, held his gaze a moment before blushing and looking away. Slowly she sat back and regarded him again.

Even their silence was electrifying. Another flash of heat surged through Donovan, compelling him to taste her lips. He pecked her lips once. Then again. The third time, a hankering pounded in his chest. Donovan wrapped his arms around her and pulled her close. Chloe's hands found his chest, then meandered to the back of his head and neck. She held him tight. With his strong arms, he drew her closer to him.

When his erection strained against his jeans, he pulled away, unable to stay another moment. He didn't want to completely lose control. She had to be ready for him.

Sitting back, Donovan panted. "I'll let myself out. See you Tuesday?"

"No."

Donovan looked at her questioningly. "No?" Why was she suddenly saying no about Tuesday? he wondered.

"No need to let yourself out." Chloe stared directly into his eyes. "I don't want you to go."

Donovan understood. He understood everything in that moment. "You sure about this?"

Chloe nodded. Her parted lips spoke of her longing. Donovan covered her mouth with his, swiping the pillows to the ground. He unleashed a passion so intense when his lips connected with hers that it was blinding.

Donovan lay on top of her, careful not to trap her under the weight of his body. Drawing back from their kiss, he stared at her for a moment, questioning her with his eyes.

Chloe's response was another kiss, giving license to take this to the next level. Her slim fingers skillfully unbuttoned his shirt.

Donovan fought his body's reaction to her hands on his bare chest. This woman had no idea of her effect on him. Chloe pushed his shirt back at his shoulders. He let her take it off and watched as she reached for his belt buckle. He refused to move, allowing her actions to serve as con-

firmation and authorization. His erection sprung forward
when she zipped down his pants. Chloe's eyes widened
at his size, though he was still hidden behind his boxers.

Donovan lifted her shirt over her head, admired her
lace bra a moment before unsnapping it from the back. He
palmed her breasts—some of the prettiest he'd ever seen.

Chloe stood. Donovan unbuttoned her jeans and shim-
mied them past her hips. The bra matched the panties.
He leaned forward and circled her navel with his tongue.
Chloe's back arched and her breath caught.

Stepping out of her jeans she held her hand out. Donovan took it, stood and let her lead him to her bedroom—
a cozy space with a romantic monochromatic décor in
varying shades from ivory to tan. The chandelier over the
queen-sized bed gave the room a majestic feel.

Donovan backed Chloe up against the end of her bed
and gently laid her down. He put his finger to her lips.

"Are you sure?"

Chloe nodded.

Starting at her forehead, Donovan kissed a trail to her
feet, getting acquainted with every inch of her. Chloe
rubbed Donovan's head when he reached her lower parts,
hissing from his exploration. Donovan rose to her upper
half, taking her nipples gently between his teeth. Chloe's
back arched and a sweet, small moan lodged in her throat.
Donovan could sense it. When he had his feel of her
mounds, he slid down to her navel before spreading her
legs to truly taste her.

Donovan framed her folds with his hands before sinking
his face into her moist center. Teasing her bud, he flicked
his tongue over the tip. Chloe jerked away. Donovan chuckled, adoring her response, and did it again and again. She
retreated slightly each time and moaned. He covered her
button with the cushion of his lips and gently sucked until
she writhed, grappled at his head and chanted his name.

"Oh my… Donovan. Oh!"

Lifting up, he took her in his arms, letting her buck against him as her release held her rigidly hostage. Before her body could relax, he sheathed himself and slid inside of her folds. She received him well, wrapped him in her warm cocoon. Her walls were still clenched, holding him like suction.

Donovan swallowed hard, attempting to delay the effects of her. He moved in further, slowly at first, and found a sweet rhythm and rode it until he felt close to exploding. Her soft moans were music, yet compelled him. Donovan pulled out.

"No!" Chloe said breathlessly, reaching for him.

Donovan counted to ten and entered her again. He regained control. She shuddered when he reached her all the way on the inside. Stoking easily, Donovan watched her facial contortions caused by the delicious pleasure they created together.

Donovan felt pressure building at the base of his erection and knew he wouldn't last much longer. Veins protruded in his arms and the friction between them intensified. He couldn't hold back this time. Thrusting against her, he grunted.

"Chloe!" he gasped as if to warn her.

"Donovan!" Her voice squeaked. Chloe grappled at his chest and then grabbed his hips, guiding his plunges deeper inside of her.

Chloe's back arched hard and she groaned. Donovan's core tightened. His back hunched with tension. At the same time, they called each other's name. Donovan's rhythm increased, no longer under his control. His release barreled through him in waves, taking his unyielding body hostage. Every jolt crippled him a little more.

Finally, the climax let go of its firm hold on him. Chloe calling his name sounded like desperate pleas before she collapsed. Their warm sweaty bodies lay entangled until they were able to bring their breathing under control. They lay in each other's arms, basking in their exhilaration.

Donovan already knew he wouldn't be able to get enough of Chloe. Round two turned into three, leaving them spent.

The banging on Chloe's front door coupled with the incessant ringing startled them both awake. Neither had realized they'd fallen asleep. Moreover, she seemed just as surprised as him that daylight had found them still naked and wrapped in each other's arms.

The banging started again. The doorbell chimed once more. Chloe wrapped a sheet around her and ran to the bedroom window.

Her gasps made Donovan spring out of bed and run to her. She looked at him as dread washed over her face. "It's my mother!"

your phone. When I couldn't get you again this morning, I came right over and here you are still in your pajamas." El huffed. One hand held her purse and the other was parked on her hip. She looked exasperated.

"I'm sorry, Mom." Chloe looked left and then right. "Where is my cell phone?"

El sucked her teeth. "See what I mean? You had us worried sick."

Chloe pushed the wisps of hair that had fallen over her eye out of the way and headed to the den, looking for her phone. She'd left it on the coffee table next to the chessboard. She heard her mother's steps growing closer. Chloe grabbed her cell and met her mother in the hall. She didn't want her to see the chessboard, the open wine bottle and near empty glasses and start asking questions.

"Here it is." She forced her voice to sound surprised.

"Humph." El pursed her sweetheart lips. Her coral lipstick creased. Even with her skeptical glare, she was pretty with her shoulder-length hair and sharp-looking business dress. "I called to tell you that Jacqueline Bosley was at the restaurant last night while we were having dinner at home with the family."

"Jacqueline Bosley, the famous actress?" Chloe's brows wrinkled. "Nice."

"Yes. *The* Jacqueline Bosley." El moved toward the kitchen. Chloe looked toward the steps again and followed her. "Karen called me. Apparently, she enjoyed the food and thought the service impeccable. I believe that may be the result of your working with…those women. You know the ones who worked with…" El paused as if she couldn't dare say the Rivers name.

Chloe thought about Donovan being upstairs and cringed. "That's great, Mom." She tried to sound enthused.

El searched Chloe's refrigerator and retrieved a bottle of spring water. She walked over to the cabinet and took

Chapter 15

Chloe finger-combed her tousled hair. Frantically, she flung clothes from the drawers in her closet until she found a long T-shirt she often wore to bed. Donovan sat calmly at the edge of her bed. The doorbell and the knocks were still sounding off. She could hear El calling out her name.

Chloe ran down the steps, almost plunging to the bottom. Before opening the door, she ran to the den and kicked the clothes that she and Donovan had shed the night before under the couch. Pushing her hair back again, she headed for the door, pulling it open. She squinted as the sunlight assaulted her eyes.

"What happened to you?" El stepped around her and entered the house.

Chloe looked toward the stairs. "Nothing!" Chloe looked past her mother to the outside. "Is Daddy with you? Is something wrong?" Chloe was suddenly filled with alarm at the thought of something bad happening to her father.

"Dad's fine. I'm here to find out what happened to you." El looked around as if she were looking for clues.

Chloe was able to breathe knowing that her dad was fine. "Oh." Chloe's hand was at her heart. She didn't remember putting it there. "I'm fine. Why wouldn't I be?"

"For one, you've been acting strange lately. I've be~~~ trying to call you since last night and you never ans~~~

out a glass, screwed the top off the water bottle and poured the water in the glass. El would never be caught drinking from a bottle, regardless of what was inside.

Chloe started wringing her hands and stopped, clasping them behind her. She looked at the ceiling, praying Donovan would stay put while she tried to get rid of her mother. She looked up to catch El staring at her.

"What time is it?" Chloe squinted toward the time on the microwave. "Oh! It's already eight o'clock. I need to get dressed. Mom, I'll see you at the office."

El drank another sip of water, huffed and shook her head. "What's up with you?"

"Nothing. I just..." A lie wouldn't come quickly enough. "I have a lot on my mind with this event I'm working on, that's all."

There was a thump against the ceiling. Chloe's and El's heads snapped upward at the same time.

"What was that?" El put her glass down and went to walk out of the kitchen to investigate.

"Mom!"

El spun around. "What?"

"That was probably the book I was reading in bed. I feel asleep in the middle of it. I must have knocked it to the edge of the bed when I jumped out to come down and answer the door for you. I'll get it when I get back upstairs." Chloe was talking too much.

Now El's gaze was penetrating.

Chloe pushed out a yawn. "I'm exhausted. I need a good shower to wake me up. I'll meet you at the office." She walked to the door though she didn't hear her mother's steps behind her.

Chloe's hand was poised to turn the knob and El still hadn't moved. El looked up at the ceiling one last time. She clucked her tongue and finally progressed toward the door. Relief shrouded Chloe. She yawned one more time, continuing her performance—though it was possibly poor. She was good at singing and never claimed to act.

"Hurry up! We've got a lot to talk about," El said as she walked through the door.

"I'm jumping in the shower right now."

The second El stepped out, Chloe closed the door and locked it. She ran to the window to watch her mother climb into her Mercedes-Benz and then waited for her to take off.

Chloe bolted up the stairs, ready to yell at Donovan about that sound she'd heard, but stopped in her tracks when she saw his still naked body lying on the bed with his hands behind his head. Her eyes zeroed in on his slightly hardened member.

Donovan lifted onto his elbows. "I was going to get dressed but most of my clothes are downstairs. Then I thought that you might need a little something to calm your nerves once your mom left so I didn't want to put him away." Donovan looked down at his growing erection, smiled and looked back at Chloe.

Chloe shook her head and chuckled. "I can't believe this." She rested her hand on her forehead and noticed her heartbeat had yet to slow down.

Donovan sat up and patted the bed next to him. Chloe sat beside him.

"What fell?" she asked, remembering the noise.

"Me," Donovan admitted.

"What? How?" Chloe's forehead creased.

"I tried to get to the bathroom in case your mother came upstairs and slipped on the sheet you left on the floor. I don't usually have to hide like that. I haven't done something like that since I was a teenager."

At first, Chloe sat blank-faced. Although Donovan smiled as he spoke, she sensed a hint of seriousness. When he starting laughing, Chloe joined him and found that she couldn't stop. The craziness of her situation and her frazzled nerves made her delirious. Eventually, she leaned over and kissed Donovan, appreciating the sacrifices he had made for her sake.

"Thank you."

They kissed again which led to another round of love-making before showering together.

"Chloe," Donovan called out, as they were about to enter their cars.

"Yes." She couldn't read his expression as he walked back over to her.

"I'm not interested in keeping us a secret." His eyes bore into hers, finishing his statement for him.

Chloe blinked rapidly, cleared her throat and squeaked out a small, "Okay," which sounded more like a question. She understood the unspoken part of his statement clearly. Donovan wanted more and if she wanted more, too, she'd have to stop acting like a rebellious teen and take a mature stand.

Donovan bent forward and gave her one last kiss before leaving her dumbfounded. Chloe watched him enter the car, start the engine and drive away until she couldn't see him anymore, then she got in her vehicle and drove off.

On the way to work, her thoughts vacillated between the previous night and El's surprise appearance. She heard Donovan's comment over and over. He wasn't interested in keeping them a secret anymore. While that flattered the heck out of her, it also frightened her. Would dating Donovan seriously be worth all the conflict it would cause? Chloe hated conflict. She called Jewel.

"Did you speak to Mom yet?" Jewel asked straightaway.

"Did I?" Chloe filled Jewel in on everything that happened in the past fifteen hours. Jewel whooped, hollered, screamed and cackled throughout the entire account.

"Oh my good Lord up in heaven." Jewel laughed. "What are you going to do?"

"I don't know." Chloe groaned, stretching each word.

"First of all, do you like him?"

Chloe whined. "Yes. I do." She exhaled, feeling as though weight dissipated when she admitted the truth. "I honestly do. I thought this would just be a fun rendezvous— a chance to do something different. I never expected to feel this way about him. It's like he tapped into a version of me that's been buried for years and now that she's out, I don't want her to go away." Chloe snickered.

Jewel squealed. "That sounds so romantic. So you have no choice."

"What do you mean?"

"You have to tell the family—well, tell Mom. She's the only one that would have an issue. If this is what you want, stand up for it. She'll understand—eventually," Jewel said as if it were as easy to do.

"This is our mom you're talking about. Ms. Elnora Chandler. Have you met her?" Chloe's sarcasm made Jewel laugh. "The whole thought of that gives me heartburn." Chloe thumped her chest with her fist.

"It doesn't have to be today but it needs to happen soon. Most men wouldn't be willing to wait too long. I imagine it's a bit of a blow to his ego as well."

Chloe had never thought about that. For weeks, Chloe and Donovan had been spending time together as if they were in a serious relationship. Last night definitely took things to another level. However, they never actually talked about putting a label on what they were doing.

"I'll call you back." Chloe ended the call before Jewel could respond. She had so much to think about now. She needed to have a serious talk with Donovan. They would have that talk tonight over dinner.

When Chloe reached Chandlers, she could tell something was up. Karen, their restaurant and catering manager, had a strained look on her face, the way it did when

El was uptight. Her mother's mood had a way of permeating the entire staff. Chloe often tried to lighten the atmosphere when her mother got like this.

Chloe marched right to her mother's office but she wasn't there. She headed to her own office and bumped right into her.

"You finally made it. Come to my office." El grabbed Chloe by the hand. "There's so much going on. We have a deal on the table and it needs to happen the right way." El sat and searched through papers on her desk. "Where are those ladies you were working with? Maybe we need to call a meeting with them." She lifted her head toward her open office door. "Karen, I need you. Get me the number to MarComm, right away."

Chloe looked at her mother confused. She hadn't been able to get a word in yet.

"Mom," Chloe called her name.

"There's a meeting today. Last minute, but we need to be prepared." El found the paper she was searching for and reached for her desk phone but stopped midway. She put the paper in front of Chloe.

"Mom."

"Take a look at this. If we don't have time to talk to MarComm before we leave, we need to figure out what to present."

"Mom!" Chloe shouted. "What's this all about?"

El's head snapped up. She looked at Chloe as if she'd seen her for the first time. She put her hand to her forehead. "Oh dear! I'm frantic."

"Yes, you are. What's going on?"

El looked at her watch. "Jacqueline Bosley wants to do an event here." El jabbed a finger on her mahogany desk. "Here! Can you believe that? She has a foundation and wants to host their annual benefit here. At Chandlers. She asked for a meeting. We need to be in her office at noon."

Chloe understood. Chandlers had done well and hosted many events for the prominent people across Long Island, including local celebrities. Some of them were friends of the Chandlers, but having an A-list actress like Jacqueline Bosley do an event at their venue would take their business to a new dimension. The exposure would be life changing.

El didn't come undone about much but she was clearly elated about the opportunity. It wasn't often that the consumer goods industry crossed paths with Hollywood in this way.

"Okay. I'll grab the materials on our different packages. We can go over what we'd like to offer before we get there. I'll be back." Chloe headed to her office, happy that she had a reason to put this situation with Donovan on the back burner for a while. She loved having new projects that she could delve into.

For the next hour, El and Chloe deliberated over what to offer Jacqueline Bosley and came up with a package they were both pleased with. They agreed to go all out with what they would propose, believing that only the best would do for the likes of Jacqueline. Details made the difference in situations like this.

The two arrived at the office of The Jacqueline Bosley Foundation a few minutes early. The office was located in a storefront on a main strip in The Hamptons. It shared the block with galleries, swank eateries, coffee bars and upscale clothing boutiques. A young receptionist with large brown eyes ushered them to the rear of the rectangular-shaped space into a conference room and promised that Jacqueline would be with them shortly. Pictures of Jacqueline with dignitaries, politicians and other actors adorned the wall alongside images of her with children surrounding her in different theatrical settings.

From what Chloe had researched, Jacqueline's foundation funded organizations that served underserved youth through the arts. Jacqueline had come from troubled meager beginnings and credited a local theater arts program for turning her life around and setting her on the path to success. She was committed to making a similar impact in the lives of young people who saw theater arts as a way out. The foundation was fairly new and this gala would be the second of its kind. The first was held in New York City and was well attended by Hollywood actors supporting the cause.

Jacqueline stepped in the room and for a moment Chloe paused. Never one to be starstruck, Chloe was still captured by Jacqueline's raw beauty and kind eyes. Shapely and svelte, Jacqueline had thick brown hair that flowed endlessly. She moved like liquid in a way that was almost mesmerizing.

"Thank you for coming. I'm Jacqueline." She stretched out her hand. "This is Marie Blakely. She is the executive director of my foundation and handles things in my absence. However, for this particular event, I will speak directly with you. This gala is my pride and joy. It's my pleasure to take this on—especially now that I have some downtime."

El stood, straightening to her fully refined self. With her head lifted high and a welcoming but tight smile, she shook Jacqueline's and Marie's hands in turn. "Pleasure to meet you. This is a lovely office you have here."

"Yes." Chloe shook Jacqueline's hand. "We're excited to show you what we have to offer."

"Wonderful and please call me Jackie." She sauntered over to the head of the table. "We're just waiting on a few others." Jacqueline sat as languidly as she walked. "I did some investigating this past month and identified several locations that I wanted to consider for my gala. Your place, which by the way has the most delicious food—" Jacqueline smiled "—is one of my top three choices. You're a little early but the other two should be here shortly."

El smiled but Chloe knew she wasn't happy about what she'd just heard. The fact that El hadn't mentioned competition meant she wasn't aware of it. That bit of information would have affected their preparation for this meeting. Chloe wondered who the other companies were.

The receptionist walked in with the owners of the second place, The Crest, a beautiful place near the water as well. They greeted each other cordially and shook hands. Jacqueline gestured for them to sit on the opposite side of the conference table and they all engaged in small talk.

Several minutes later, they heard the receptionist approach with several footsteps accompanying her. A familiar voice lifted into the air and El froze. Jacqueline stood as the door opened.

"Ah, yes. It looks like we're ready to start. Please have a seat." She gestured for the two who just entered to sit at the other end of the table.

Greetings didn't flow as cordially as it had when the second owners arrived. In fact, they almost didn't flow at all when El stood and faced Joliet Rivers with Donovan at her side. Chloe swallowed hard and tried to maintain a professional demeanor.

"Elnora Chandler," Joliet said with surprise.

"Joliet Rivers," El said with slight disdain.

Donovan stepped toward Chloe and shook her hand. "Chloe." He nodded his greeting. A jolt of energy surged through her hands.

"Donovan." She barely recognized her own voice. Chloe pulled her hand from his but his eyes remained on her long after greetings made their way around the room and the meeting officially began.

Chloe wanted to disappear.

Chapter 16

Joliet paced for the better part of the day. El's presence at the meeting had obviously perturbed her. Since their return to the office, she'd been off kilter.

Donovan walked into her office to catch her staring toward the window. Beyond the pane was a lush golf course but he was certain that Joliet wasn't taking it in.

"Mom," he called softly and took a seat in the chair across from her desk.

"Yes…yes, dear?" He'd drawn her in from some faraway place.

"Want to tell me what the deal is between our family and the Chandlers?"

Joliet nervously pushed documents around her desk. "That's not important, dear. Getting that contract…" She pointed at him. "That's important. Have you taken a look at any numbers based on our conversation? We have a week to present our package and I want to make sure that nothing is overlooked."

Donovan sighed. "Once you've determined everything you want in the package, I can work out the numbers."

"Great! This will be excellent exposure for La Belle Riviere. We have to get this." Joliet picked up the phone and called the catering manager. "Harry? Hi. Any progress on that menu? It has to be impressive…Okay…Wonderful…Let me know as soon as it comes in." Joliet put the phone down and sat back. Her red lips pressed together and her brow furrowed the way they often did when she was deep in thought.

Donovan stood. "Let me know when you get the information from Harry. We should probably call a meeting for Wednesday maybe. All departments should be able to have their parts worked out by then and we can finalize our numbers by Thursday. That will be more than enough time to lay out something impressive for Jacqueline."

"Sounds good, dear." Joliet was dismissive, which was weird since normally she and Donovan often had great camaraderie.

Donovan headed back to his office. He tried Chloe's number again. There was still no answer. She hadn't picked up her phone or responded to her texts since their meeting earlier. He could tell by her expression at the meeting that she and her mother were as shocked as they were. The timing couldn't have been worse but with the way he felt about Chloe, he didn't plan to give up.

After work, he drove by Chloe's to see if her car was there. He dialed her number after spotting her car in the driveway.

"Can I come in?" he asked when she picked up.

Chloe paused for a moment before saying yes.

Chloe opened the door and Donovan kissed her as he usually did. Without saying much, Chloe headed for the kitchen. He followed behind her. The atmosphere had shifted dramatically since he'd been there earlier that morning. Neither of them could have anticipated the day they'd had. Donovan was sure El was acting just as strangely as Joliet had.

"What a day," Chloe said, opening a pan releasing a fragrant aroma.

"Yeah." Donovan sat on one of the stools at the island.

"Jacqueline was really pouring it on today." Donovan sensed a twinge of jealousy from Chloe and he liked it.

"What? Pfft?" Donovan waved dismissively.

Chloe stopped flipping the fish in the pan. "Don't act like you didn't recognize Jacqueline flirting with you. Everyone at the table could see it even if we were all legally blind."

"It wasn't that obvious," Donovan said with a mischievous grin.

"Oh, come on. She kept staring at you as if she were about to take a bite in front of everyone. I saw her batting those lashes at you. And when we were leaving, she practically stripped you with those bedroom eyes. 'It was such a pleasure to meet you, Donovan.'" Chloe swayed, mocking Jacqueline with exaggerated flair. She batted her eyes excessively and laughed. "I thought she was going to jump your bones before we left there."

"Hey! Can you blame her?" Donovan straightened, tugged on his collar confidently and winked.

"Whatever, hotshot." Chloe gave him a sideways glance. "Just don't try to use that to your advantage to get this deal. I need to win this contract fair and square."

Donovan shielded his body with his arms as if he were ashamed. "I feel like a piece of meat," he whined jokingly. Donovan laughed with Chloe and shook his head. "How's your mother doing?" he asked, happy to change the subject.

Chloe groaned. "She's been on a rampage. I had to call my father to get her to calm down a little. She feels like she'd been blindsided. I told her there was no way that Jacqueline Bosley could have known about her and your mother's strained relationship. What about your mom?"

"Nuts." Donovan popped a piece of carrot that Chloe had been cutting for the salad into his mouth. "It makes me wonder what happened between them."

"My mother refuses to tell us." Chloe scooped the remaining carrots into a dish and proceeded to cut other vegetables.

"Mine, too."

Chloe shook her head. "Hungry?" she asked without lifting her head.

"Smells amazing. I couldn't say no if I wanted to."

Chloe added strawberries and pecans to the salad and began plating it. She laid thick pieces of salmon next to the salad and poured two glasses of tea. For moments they ate in silence.

"Have you thought about what I said this morning?"

"I thought about it all day," Chloe said, scooping a forkful of salad. "Especially after this afternoon's fiasco."

"Well?"

Chloe sat back. "I don't know what to do. Mentioning this to my mother right now wouldn't turn out well."

"I understand. We can wait until after next week's meeting with the foundation. Once that is out of the way, things should settle a bit." Donovan sipped his tea and wiped his mouth with a cloth napkin. For a moment, he stared at Chloe as she ate.

Somewhere along the line, she'd opened him up to the possibility of serious dating once again. When they saw one another in Puerto Rico, he thought it was a good opportunity to indulge the curiosity he'd had about her since their high-school days. He assumed the most that would happen was that they might have a rendezvous like Jewel and his brother.

What Donovan hadn't expected was to admire her so much. He couldn't have predicted that being with her would feel like just the right fit in so many ways.

At this point, he wasn't interested in playing games with her or their families. The past few weeks showed him that he wanted to be with her and it didn't matter who had an issue with that. Yet he understood her position and didn't mind giving it another week. After that, he wanted to claim his girl and didn't care what anyone had to say about it.

Donovan wouldn't push this issue tonight. In fact, he wanted things between them to feel normal again. They'd made significant strides in recent weeks—especially last night. He wanted to get back to that euphoric place they had arrived at this morning before El came knocking on Chloe's door.

"Delicious!" Donovan sat back, feeling sated. "I have a nice after-dinner wine in my car. Let me run and get it."

"Sounds good." Chloe answered him shortly.

Donovan was about to change her attitude. He grabbed the prized bottle of wine from his trunk and returned quickly. Knowing where she kept things by now, he pulled an opener from the drawer and grabbed two glasses, pouring a little wine in each.

"Taste it." He held one up to her. "Tell me what you think."

Chloe put her fork down and took the glass. She swirled it, sniffed it and put it to her lips. Letting it roll around her tongue, she looked at Donovan smiling approvingly as she swallowed.

"Exquisite. It reminds me of an ice wine I once had in Canada."

"Great palate. That's exactly what it is. One of my favorites." Donovan poured more in each glass. "I think it would go well with a good, fair game of chess."

"Fair!" Chloe narrowed her eyes at him. "Are you trying to say our other games weren't fair?"

Donovan didn't say anything with words, but said all he needed with his lifted brow and skeptical sneer.

Chloe slid off her stool, scraped her plate clean in the garbage and set it in the sink. She turned to Donovan and clapped her hands. "I think it's time to beat that denial out of you. Shall we?" Chloe waved her hand toward the den.

"Ladies first." Donovan swept his arm before her, stepped back and made room for her to pass.

"Humph! I can't believe you think I cheated. It kills me that men can never believe when they've been crushed honestly. I'll just have to beat you until you know for certain that I am simply the master."

Donovan smiled at all her trash talking, happy to have shifted her mood. "That's if you win tonight."

"Oh, I'll win all right! Bring that great-tasting wine in here. You'll need it to soothe the pain of defeat."

Two games later and Chloe was still the undefeated champion. Donovan shook his head, awed by her skills.

"Are you a believer now, Mr. Rivers?"

"I let you win again." He smirked.

Chloe tossed a pillow from the couch at him. "Liar!"

Donovan caught the pillow and cast it aside. "You'll never know, now will you?"

"One last game. This should seal the cap on all that unbelief. There's no reason you should be in denial after this next game."

"I'm done being a gentleman. I won't let you win this time." Donovan set the pieces on the board.

Chloe's mouth fell open. She scooted to the edge of the couch. "You go first, Mr. Sore Loser."

He loved fueling her trash talk.

"It won't matter."

"Watch closely. Maybe you'll learn something," he continued to tease, still awed by how well she played.

"What? How to lose sorely? Ha!" Chloe taunted him through the entire game and once again came out victorious. "Checkmate!" she yelled, thrusting two fists in the air and standing on her feet. "Are you a believer now? Huh?" She threw her head back and released a fake evil laugh.

Donovan laughed, grabbed her arm and pulled her down on top of him. "You may win at chess but let's see who wins this contract. Business is my forte." Their mouths were inches apart.

Chloe smiled slickly. "Mine, too. I've never been scared of a little competition."

The temperature between them increased significantly. Donovan's eyes went to her lips, admiring their plumpness. He licked his lips in anticipation of tasting hers. He stole a kiss. "Get your tricks ready because I have a few of my own."

"I play and win fairly every time," Chloe whispered seductively.

Donovan could feel her breath as she spoke. Heat spread throughout Donovan's groin.

"So do I, but I never show my opponent my hand." Donovan winked. Chloe squinted at him. "Feel like kissing my wounds?" he teased.

Chloe tittered, shaking her head. Donovan covered her mouth with his and kissed with all the passion he'd been holding back since she stood so close to him. Chloe sat up and pulled her shirt over her head. Donovan pushed her bra over her mounds and flicked his tongue across her nipples. She arched and moaned. Donovan took his shirt off and they helped one another out of their pants.

"Come here." Donovan's voice was low and husky. He gently laid her on the couch and traced a finger along her skin from head to toe. Chloe squirmed underneath him. Her anticipation made him more eager.

Parting her thighs, Donovan buried his face in her center and lapped until she breathlessly called his name. She tried to scamper from his reach. He held on tighter, suckling her bud until her body convulsed repeatedly and an erotic chant flitted from her trembling lips. Sitting up on the couch, he guided Chloe in front of him.

"Wait!" she said, lowering herself to his erection. She

took him into her mouth. He hissed. His body bucked involuntarily.

Chloe cushioned his erection with the walls of her mouth, nearly sending him over a quick edge. Gently, he pushed her back. She looked up at him.

"I want to feel you," he whispered.

Donovan guided her. Chloe straddled him. He eased inside of her. The intense pleasure caused both of their heads to fall back. They spoke joy in moans. Up and down she sprung. He steered her with his hands on her hips. They moved faster. Their tempo increased along with their need. Chloe bounced harder. Donovan met her thrust for thrust.

Hungry for one another, their hands roamed every exposed part of each other's body. Erotic resonances filled the room. *Ah*s, moans, skin against skin. They moved faster until the sensation became too delicious to bear.

Donovan grunted long and loud. Chloe followed up with a shriek. Donovan felt his muscles tighten just before an explosion ripped through him. His eyes squeezed shut. His final groan was guttural. Chloe collapsed against his chest, her lower walls clenching and unclenching his fading erection. Donovan wrapped his arms around her. They clung to each other desperately—a sweaty, entangled, sated heap.

Donovan had managed to end the night just the way he had planned—with Chloe in his arms.

Chapter 17

"**W**hat's gotten into you?" El stood in the doorway to Chloe's office with her arms folded and her lips pursed. "What's going on?"

"What do you mean?" Chloe feigned innocence.

"I'm here going crazy over this package we're preparing for Jacqueline and you're prancing around here humming like you're completely unfazed."

"Humming?" Chloe looked confused.

"Yes, humming! Don't you even hear yourself?"

The smile Chloe had been trying to hold back escaped. "I didn't even realize it." Thoughts of the sensual things Donovan did to her that morning flashed in her mind. Just thinking of the past few days while she looked at her mother's furrowed brows made her blush. If El could read minds, she'd lose hers.

El huffed, dismissing Chloe's strange behavior. "Just come to my office. Karen acquired the information from last year's benefit that we were looking for."

"Oh. That's great! Give me one minute to finish up this email and I'll be right there."

El continued eyeing Chloe with a narrowed gaze for a moment longer before dropping her arms. "All right. Hurry up. I want to get through this as early as possible."

Chloe's phone dinged. It was another text message from Donovan that generated a joyous laugh from her core.

Chloe shook her head and tapped out a response. Even after several nights of multiple beatings at chess, Donovan still refused to admit defeat. He seemed to enjoy getting whipped by her. Chloe thought about letting him win at least one game of chess for the sake of his ego.

Chloe truly enjoyed the time they spent together playing chess, going out and visiting jazzy lounges across Manhattan. She'd become quite the underground celebrity. "Her audience," as she had come to think about them, came with requests each week. Their mutual adoration filled her heart and fed her ego.

The previous Tuesday evening, she'd responded to a request by singing her own arrangement of a heartfelt song by India Arie. The beautiful song spoke of a father's request to let his children know he was a good man.

Chloe was so caught up in the performance that she didn't remember singing anything after the first verse. It was as if she'd blacked out. When she released the last eloquent note, she looked over the crowd that was silent at first. Tears flowed from her eyes as well as several audience members. One by one they stood, blessing her with a standing ovation. She bowed humbly before walking off the stage right into the arms of Donovan. He had begun calling Chloe his butterfly that night, referring to the way singing spawned a metamorphosis.

Chloe allowed herself to wonder about the surprise Donovan had planned for her this coming Friday evening before steering her thoughts back to the present.

Chloe exhaled, grabbed her cell phone and the journal she kept for her notes and headed to her mother's office. She was the last to arrive at the meeting. El, Karen their catering manager and Nayda the administrative assistant all sat waiting on her.

"Let's get started right away," El instructed. "Karen, please share your findings."

"Sure." She turned toward Chloe. "I did some research and found the venue that Jacqueline held her gala at last year. I called over and 'made nice' with the catering manager and asked a few questions. She filled me in on a few things that she said really mattered to Jacqueline and gave me some tips on how we could potentially impress her in our package."

"Good stuff, Karen." El shifted in her seat and nodded approvingly. "What are some of those details?" she urged.

"For one thing, Jacqueline absolutely loves lilies," Karen announced. "We need to make sure those are part of what we offer for the tables and decor. As extravagant as she appears, Jacqueline really prefers simple elegance, nothing too overdone. Monochromatic decorative themes work well for her. She's a vegetarian and delicious offerings for her guests are important. She's big on nature and visual elements. We need to make sure we amplify the views of the pier and the fact that we can open up this side of the room facing the marina to allow the sights and sounds of the water in." Karen directed her attention to El. "I have a few great new recipes that I'd like to run by you for some of those vegetarian options."

"Nice job with your investigation, Karen," Chloe said genuinely. "Can you work with the chefs and whip up a few samples for us to take with us to taste before our meeting?"

"Sure. We can start this afternoon when he gets in," Karen said.

"Great! Let's get some swatches of fabric and a mock-up of a few decorative options for the meeting as well. We also really need to put a big focus on the view in this presentation. Let's gather all the images that really show it off," El said.

"It sounds like we'll only need to make a few enhancements to our current offerings to make this an impressive package," Chloe added. She sat back feeling confident. She wondered how Donovan would respond to getting beat out of this contract. Chloe placed her hand to her chin to hide her smile, making it look like she was thinking.

"I wish I knew what the others were presenting. The Rivers' food isn't as good as ours anyway." El punctuated her statement with an arrogant flip of her hair. "The only thing they have going for them is the fact that their property is adjacent to the golf course. I have to admit, it does provide stunning views of rolling greens and lush landscaping. Our place has more personality and it seems that Jacqueline would value that. The pier is so picturesque with the water, yachts and all. I believe our place is simply a better fit. We just have to get Jacqueline to see that." El snapped closed the journal she'd been using to write notes in and sat back as if her statement would make this a done deal.

"What about the owners of The Crest?" Karen asked.

"I'm not concerned about them. Their place is nice but it's no more interesting than any other catering hall with overdone fountains and chandeliers. One could get that anywhere. But our pier…" El lifted her chin even higher. "Not many others can offer the beauty and essence of being near the water. Heck! At this point, I don't even count them as competition." El narrowed her eyes in a calculating manner. "But those Rivers…they're another story. We have to beat them out!" she said pointedly.

Chloe resisted the urge to roll her eyes. "Karen, you work on the menu. I'll work on the swatches, fabrics and putting together the visual package. Let's meet again on Friday morning and see what we have to work with."

"Call up our florist and tell him we'll need the most exotic lilies he can find for the event. Let's bring a few to the meeting," El said, directing her pen in Karen's direction.

"Great idea, Mom."

"Of course it is!" El declared.

Chloe's phone rang and Donovan's name flashed across the screen. She nearly knocked her notes to the floor trying to grab her phone before anyone else could see the name. Chloe texted that she was in a meeting and would call him back momentarily and then placed her phone back on the table facedown.

El looked at the overturned phone and looked up at Chloe. Her eyes were filled with scrutiny.

"We're off to a great start. I need to get back to work now. We still have this reception to prepare for and there's still so much to be done." Chloe stood to exit her mother's office.

"Chloe," El called just before she reached the door.

"Yes." Chloe turned back to her mother and smiled.

"I haven't seen much of you outside of work lately. Your sisters don't seem to know what's going on with you, either."

Chloe felt as if her mother was looking right through her. "Actually," she fumbled a little and cleared her throat. "I've been at home taking in some me time. That's all. I'm really enjoying it." She hated lying to her mother. In time she'd tell everything.

"Oh. Well, you do work pretty hard. I thought maybe you met someone and was keeping him in hiding. I figured something had you humming. I guess a little recharging can do that for you."

"It sure can." An image of her walking into Donovan's arms flashed across her mind. Chloe turned to leave.

"Well, your father and I haven't seen much of you lately." Chloe turned back as El continued speaking. "Come to the house for dinner Sunday? It will be nice. Just the family, you know?"

"Sure. That sounds nice." Chloe smiled. Donovan

wanted to cook for her on Sunday. She was beginning to see how keeping him as her salacious little secret could soon become challenging.

Chapter 18

"Donovan, darling!" Joliet whizzed into his office.

Her startling entrance snatched his attention, but before he could respond verbally, words began to tumble from her mouth.

"Your father just called. He had an accident on the golf course earlier. Instead of going straight to the doctor, he went home." Joliet paced quickly. "Now his ankle is, as he describes, as big as a basketball. I could tell he was in pain by the sound of his voice." Worry deepened the lines in her beautiful almond-colored face. "I'm heading there now to get him and take him to the emergency room. I'm supposed to meet with Jacqueline Bosley tonight." Her hand slapped her forehead. "She called this morning to set it up."

"Another meeting? Why?" he asked.

Joliet stopped moving, tapered her eyes and looked sideways. "Did I forget to mention this to you?" She waved dismissively. Her verbal stampede continued without giving Donovan a chance to answer. "She's leaning toward booking with us and wants to confirm if it's the right fit. You know those Hollywood types. It's all about the feel and the aura." Joliet waved her hand. "It's at Josephina's at six. The quaint little Italian restaurant your brother loves. I doubt we'll be out of the hospital by then but we can't afford to cancel."

"It's okay. I'll do it, Mom."

Joliet continued as if Donovan hadn't just spoken. "This could affect us getting the contract. I didn't bother asking you to join us because I know you usually go into the city on Friday evenings. She's just coming back into town and our presentations are due on Monday. I don't want to blow this. Time is of the essence here and—"

"Mom! I'll take the meeting. Go see about Dad."

"Okay!" Joliet held her hands up. "Okay. I'll call you when we get to the hospital." Joliet raced out of Donovan's office.

Seeing his refined mother so frantic was unusual. Donovan looked at his watch and closed out the file he'd been working on. It was already four thirty. Resting his head against the back of his chair, he sighed. Donovan had a special evening planned for Chloe and now that duty called, he'd have to cancel.

Reluctantly, he made all of the necessary calls to undo his plan of recreating the night they sailed in Puerto Rico. The last call he made was to Chloe to let her know that he had to cancel their plans for the night.

While he explained that the reason was due to business and his father's injury, he didn't provide details and promised to make it up to her on Sunday. Chloe's disappointment was clear, though she said she understood. Donovan assumed that, like him, Chloe had been interrogated about not being around much. Of course, it was because they spent so much time together.

The hour that Donovan spent making calls and closing out for the day went by in a flash. His mother confirmed that they'd made it to the hospital. He had just enough time to get to the restaurant with a few minutes to spare, but Jacqueline showed up a full half hour late. As one who respected people's time and preferred that his time be treated the same, he pushed aside his irritation and greeted Jacqueline with due professionalism.

"It's a pleasure to see you again, Donovan." She purred. Her handshake was more like a caress. "Will Joliet be joining us?" She moved toward the seat Donovan had pulled out for her with a fluid saunter.

Shaking his head politely, Donovan smiled. "The pleasure's all mine," he said, sitting across from her. "Unfortunately, my mother will not be able to join us. My father had a little accident and she's with him."

Jacqueline gasped. Her hand flew to her heart. "Oh no! Is he going to be okay?"

At first, Donovan was slightly taken aback by her dramatic response and wondered if she was genuinely concerned. "He injured his ankle on the golf course and it swelled pretty badly—nothing life-threatening."

"Oh! Good." Jacqueline exhaled. "I hope he feels better. Send your mother my love."

"I will."

Their waiter arrived with water and warm fresh bread that filled the atmosphere with an enticing, homey scent.

Jacqueline closed her eyes and breathed in. "Oh, that smells amazing." When she opened her eyes, she stared directly into Donovan's and smiled. "You're quite handsome, Donovan." Placing her elbows on the table, she bridged her hands and rested her chin on them. "I'll bet you drive the women around here absolutely crazy." She batted her eyes. "I imagine you must be such a playboy."

Flattered by her comment, Donovan smiled but sipped the wine the waiter had just placed in front of him instead of confirming or denying her assumption. He'd been doted on by beautiful women before. This wasn't new to him.

"My mother didn't get a chance to tell me much about this meeting. However, I can assure you that we've been working diligently on developing an impressive package for your benefit. We're sure you will be pleased," Donovan said. "Do you have any questions that I could answer for you?"

"Yes. Everything has to be perfect. I called this meeting to communicate a few important things before the final presentations. I'm specifically interested in the golf course next to your place. The views are magnificent and I'd love to do some kind of networking event over there. Perhaps the next day would be nice. It's close by and convenient. It has to feel right, you know, so I thought it would be a good idea to sit down and chat so I could gain more insight. I'm pretty close to finalizing my decision. I just need to make sure it's all a perfect fit."

Donovan successfully got the business part of the meeting on track. As they spoke, he wondered if she had additional meetings with any of the other competitors.

He appreciated how Jacqueline's demeanor took on a delightful expression when she spoke of her foundation. He could tell it meant a lot to her. Despite the significance of their conversation, she playfully touched his hands as they spoke, released freeing laughter into the air as if he'd tickled her and drew toward him as if she didn't want to miss a word. To anyone watching, it would have looked like anything but a business meeting. He answered her questions while they ate, but after a few more glasses of wine, Jacqueline's mannerism became more languid and her tongue, a bit more loose.

Leaning forward, Jacqueline made circles along the back of Donovan's hand with her slender finger. "You can't possibly be single. Right?" She managed to bring the conversation back around to him. Her eyes slowly rose from his hand to meet his eyes.

"Let's just say, I'm currently exploring a very viable option." Donovan wanted to say yes and tell her it was Chloe but knew that wouldn't turn out well for anyone. He also noticed how her touch had no effect on him. It lacked the electricity that Chloe's touch generated whenever their skin met.

Steering the conversation back to business, Donovan asked a few more questions he thought would help them seal the contract. Jacqueline responded to each inquiry but maintained her flirtatious manner.

"What are you doing after this, Donovan? I know a great bar not far from here."

"Thanks for the offer but I have to head over to the hospital to see about my father." Donovan was grateful to have a genuine reason to decline her offer. He knew he needed to handle her delicately until their business was done.

"Oh, yes!" Jacqueline slapped the table lightly. "How insensitive of me." She pouted. It looked more sexy than apologetic. With her hand to her heart, she said, "Forgive me," and arched her back, giving rise to her breasts.

Donovan chuckled. "You're forgiven." Her boldness amused him.

Jacqueline dug into her evening bag and retrieved a card. She slid it across the table to Donovan. "Please let me know how he's doing."

Donovan took the card, looked it over and stuck it in his inside pocket.

"It was a pleasure." Donovan stood, straightening his suit jacket. He held out his hand.

Jacqueline pushed his hand aside and embraced him. A moment ticked by before he hugged her back.

"A delicious meal with a handsome man is always a pleasure." Jacqueline winked and waved her fingers.

Despite wanting to maintain his distance, Donovan was a gentleman. "I'll walk you out." He stayed with her until the valet brought her car.

As stunning as Jacqueline was, the attention she poured over him had no effect. He drove to the hospital, knowing for sure that he wanted to be with Chloe.

When he arrived at his father's bedside in the emergency room, he was glad to see his parents as well as his brother. After receiving an update about his father's ankle fracture, Donovan filled them in on his meeting with Jacqueline. He could see the hope in his mother's eyes. The conversation turned back to everyday topics and suddenly, Donovan felt compelled.

"I have something I want to tell you all."

Chapter 19

"I was just about to call you," Jewel said when she answered the phone.

"About what?" Chloe asked, moving forward with their conversation and forfeiting a usual greeting. She entered her home, kicking the front door shut with her toe, and then shook her shoes off.

"Jade and I were thinking about joining you and Donovan at the lounge tonight."

"Oh! That would have been nice but we're not going." Chloe placed a bag of fresh fruit and vegetables on her kitchen counter and switched the phone from one ear to the other.

"Not going? Why?"

"Well, Donovan had planned some sort of surprise but called about an hour ago to cancel altogether. His father injured himself playing golf today and he had to handle some business for his mother while she went to see about him. After that, I think he said he was going to the hospital."

"Oh, that's too bad. I hope his dad is okay. We were really looking forward to hearing you sing. You know what? Hold on a sec." The phone went silent.

Chloe removed her purchases from the bag and placed them in the fridge one by one as she waited for Jewel to return to the line. With Donovan spending so much time

at her house, she went through food faster and found herself shopping much more often.

Chloe smiled at the half-empty carafe of cold coffee sitting on the first shelf. Donovan had taken to making coffee
for her on the evenings he was there so she wouldn't have
to stop for ice coffee every morning. Chloe had started
getting to the office a couple of minutes earlier and hadn't
been feeling so rushed.

"Chloe? Can you hear me?" Jewel asked, bringing
Chloe back to the present.

"Yes. I can hear you." Chloe shut the fridge, folded her
reusable bags and stuffed them in their designated drawer.

"Jade? Are you there?" Jewel asked.

"I'm here," Jade said.

"Good. I've got everyone! Bad news, Jade."

Jade grunted. "What is it now?"

"Chloe isn't singing tonight. She's not going into the
city at all."

"Aw! Why?"

"Something came up with Donovan," Jewel jumped in,
answering for Chloe.

"So let's go somewhere else. It's been a long time since
we've done the sister thing," Jade said.

"That's not a bad idea," Jewel replied. "Are you in,
Chloe?"

"For sure. Where should we go?" Chloe asked, now
heading to her room to change. "I need to know what to
wear."

"Can we start with dinner? I'm starving," Jade said.

"Oh! Let's go to Josephina's." Jewel's enthusiasm was
evident.

"We always go there," Jade whined.

"I can already taste that lobster scampi. Mmm." Chloe
moaned. "Come on, Jade, you know you love their tira-
misu. It's been a while since we've been there together."

"You got me there," Jade said. "Fine. Then afterward, let's go to Chris's place," she said, referring to the wine bar that their brother and two friends had just opened. "I hear they're trying out a new jazz band tonight. Maybe you could sing a little something there, Chloe. I love the name they came up with for the place, *The Reserve*. I think it's elegant," she added.

"Me, too," Chloe said, flipping through her closet with her phone propped between her ear and shoulder.

"What time should we meet?" Jewel asked.

"I told you I'm hungry. How's six thirty or seven?" Jade said.

Chloe looked at her clock. "That gives me just enough time to take a shower and find something to wear. I'm getting off the phone. See you ladies soon."

"Yay! Can't wait. I'll give Chris a call and let him know we're coming by later," Jade said.

Within the hour, Chloe was on her way to Josephina's for an overdue girls' night. She missed Donovan already but looked forward to an evening of dinner, laughs and music with her siblings. She even thought about taking to the microphone once they arrived at The Reserve just for the fun of it. Starting out a bit nervous, Chloe had come to love being onstage. The audience fueled her.

When she arrived, Jade was already there. The two waited out front for Jewel, who came speeding up the driveway, causing one of the young guys who worked the valet to two-step his way to safety. She hopped out, tossed him the keys and winked. He shook his head, jumped in Jewel's Jaguar and peeled off.

"You almost hit that boy," Chloe said.

"No, I didn't," Jewel said as if Chloe was overreacting.

Jade's wide-eyed expression showed that she agreed with Chloe. Jewel waved her off.

"Come here, silly." Jewel opened her arm and Jade

stepped into her embrace. She pulled back, holding Jade at arm's length. "Don't you look super cute? Turn around," she instructed with a twirl of her finger.

Jade sashayed in a circle showing off her couture printed leggings, flowing top and four-inch stilettos. Then she struck a runway-worthy pose with one hand on her hip. "Thanks."

Fresh out of graduate school, Jade was by far the trendiest and most daring dresser out of the three of them. Chloe kept her attire classic. Jewel loved chic ensembles with soft textures and sexy feminine lines.

They headed into the restaurant where the entire staff was familiar with them and were seated in their favorite spot, which was close to the window so they could people-watch. From their vantage point, they could also get a good look at most of the people inside the restaurant.

"So how are things going with Donovan?" Jade asked as the waitress set a carafe of Pinot Noir in the center of their table.

"You sure don't waste any time," Chloe said, picking up the glass the waiter just poured. She nodded her approval, set the glass down and the waiter filled it halfway.

"Well?" Jade sang.

Chloe blushed. "I really like him."

Jade squealed.

Jewel snickered. "I told you so."

"Whatever, Jewel." Chloe playfully rolled her eyes. "There's one problem."

Jade's expression dropped. "What's that?"

Jewel looked concerned as well.

"He's no longer interested in keeping us a secret," Chloe said. Both Jewel's and Jade's mouths dropped open.

"What are you going to do?" Jewel asked, leaning in toward Chloe.

"I don't know. I hadn't thought this far. I was having

fun and the next thing you know we started spending every available moment together. He spends the night at my house several times a week. He wants more." Chloe swallowed. "And so do I?"

"So what's the problem?"

Chloe and Jewel looked at each other and then toward Jade. "Mom!" they said in unison.

"Oh. Yeah. That." Jade grunted. "So freaking what? You're a grown woman. She'll understand or not!" Jade shrugged.

"She'd expect this from you and me," Jewel said, pointing between Jade and herself. "But never from Chloe."

"Chloe." Jade waited for Chloe to look at her. "Can you see yourself falling in love with him?"

Chloe inhaled. "I can certainly see myself falling in love with him."

Jade shrieked, then quickly covered her mouth. They laughed together, momentarily becoming the center of the restaurant's attention.

"Wait a minute!" Jewel held her hand up. "That's Jacqueline Bosley over there."

"Where?" Jade and Chloe said simultaneously. Their heads whipped in the direction Jewel pointed.

"Over there." Jewel narrowed her eyes to slits, peering across the room. "I swear that woman moves like liquid seduction."

For a moment, the three of them watched as she threw her head back, laughed and then leaned forward, making circles on the hand of the man she was sitting with.

"Wait another minute," Jewel said in disbelief. Each seemed to recognize the man she was with all at the same time. "That's…"

"Donovan…" Jade finished Jewel's sentence with a whisper.

Chloe's mouth dropped at the same time as her heart.

Her eyes were glued to their table, taking in Jacqueline's blatant flirtation. She wanted to look away but couldn't.

Jacqueline reached over and squeezed Donovan's arm, sweetly dipped her head toward her shoulder and released another carefree laugh. Donovan smiled and sipped wine.

Chloe couldn't believe what she was seeing. Here she was, contemplating for days about how to tell her mother about him, telling her sisters how she could love him and he was here with Jacqueline Bosley after lying to her about a business meeting and an injured father.

Donovan was a liar! How had she missed that? Chloe felt her heart perforating, ready to tear in pieces. She felt more hurt than she could have expected.

When Chloe finally turned around, both Jewel and Jade were staring at her, mouths slight ajar, eyes filled with concern. Her lips moved but words wouldn't form. Her appetite was gone instantly. The lobster and linguine sitting on her plate no longer looked appetizing.

"We should go," Jade whispered.

Chloe thought to go over to their table and make her presence known but remembered that Jacqueline was a potential client. She could never be so unprofessional.

Then it hit her. This could have very well been a date but Chloe suddenly knew that this had to be so much more. This was a plot to win the contract. Jacqueline had been sweet on Donovan since the moment he walked into her office that day. Chloe remembered how she would overtly peer at him in the middle of the meeting.

She decided not to say anything to Donovan at all. She'd wait and see who'd win the contract the coming week. If La Belle Riviere got it, she'd know for sure that Donovan used underhanded tactics to gain the advantage. She was almost thankful for this turn of events. It gave her a chance to see that she was about to fall for a man with marred integrity.

"Chloe," Jewel said quietly. "Are you okay?"

"I'm… I'm fine." Chloe's tone was clipped.

"I'll go ask for the bill." Jade got up and searched for their waiter.

Words didn't pass over the table until Jade returned. "The bill is taken care of. Let's go."

Chloe stood but her knees threatened to buckle. She felt her sisters' eyes on her. Swallowing, she lifted her chin and led the way to the door. Outside, they didn't even bother talking about going to The Reserve. Chloe refused their offers to come to her house. Each kissed the other, solemnly climbed into their cars and left.

Once Chloe had pulled off the restaurant's property, she allowed the dam holding her emotions to crumble. Tears slowly rolled down her cheeks as she drove home. She was upset with Donovan but also with herself for getting so caught up in him. She felt like a fool. The fact that her sisters were there to witness his betrayal made things worse.

By the time she reached her house, anger had replaced the hurt. Instead of going to her room, she headed to the study, turned on the computer and pulled up the files on the shared drive for Jacqueline's foundation gala.

Chloe caught herself fine-tuning the package to make it even more impressive, adding some of the well-received elements of her own family foundation's annual event. As usual, Chloe was able to release some of her angst by losing herself in her work. However, once she showered and laid her head on the pillow, those feelings of hurt returned.

Chloe was distraught. How would she feel the next time she saw Donovan face to face? What would she say to him? What would he say to her?

Chapter 20

Joliet hadn't taken the news well. For the remainder of the weekend, she reminded him of all the reasons why dating Chloe would be a bad idea. "What if you actually fall in love with that girl? Who'd want El as a mother-in-law? What is it about her? Why her anyway?" Joliet asked these questions and more.

Joliet had shivered at the thought of being forced into close proximity with El. "Family gatherings would be ruined. Think of what you'd have to put yourself through? You know she's evil, right?" Joliet said all of this with a straight face.

Donovan shook his head. His father shrugged. Joliet continued her protest.

Donovan had called Chloe when he left the hospital to tell her the news but she hadn't answered. In fact, she hadn't answered his calls all weekend. She did, however, text him once both Saturday and Sunday to let him know that she had family gatherings to attend.

Donovan sensed that something was wrong but couldn't confirm anything. Hearing her voice every day was something he had become used to. After going an entire weekend without speaking with her, he felt off.

Taking files from his desk, he headed to Joliet's office. Dressed in a stylish, navy blue pencil dress and her signature red lips, she looked polished and ready for business.

"Get that portfolio for me, sweetie," she said, hanging her purse from her forearm. She picked up a box with samples of their menu, being careful to hold it straight.

Donovan grabbed the portfolio as his mother had asked him. "You look nice," he said.

Joliet winked. "Thanks, darling. You have the information from Dean over at the golf course, right?"

Donovan lifted his briefcase, tilting his head in its direction. "Right here."

"Then we're all ready. Let's go."

Donovan held the doors for Joliet as they made their way to his car. Preparing for their meeting with Jacqueline had his mother on edge most of the morning. His thoughts mostly swirled around Chloe. They still hadn't spoken and he didn't have a good feeling about it. He hoped to run into her at the presentation.

Jacqueline hadn't mentioned if they were all meeting together or if she would be seeing each company separately. There wasn't much he would be able to say to Chloe at that time but at least he could see her face. Hopefully, he'd walk away with some kind of insight as to what was going on with her. Was she getting cold feet? Whatever it was, he needed to find out. Not only did her miss her voice, he also missed her touch.

Jacqueline was saying goodbye to the owners of The Crest as Joliet and Donovan walked in. Joliet and Donovan nodded politely as they left.

Jacqueline gestured for her assistant to take the box Joliet had been holding. She hugged Joliet, air kissing both sides of her face. Turning toward Donovan, she opened her arms wide and then wrapped them around Donovan. He hugged her back briefly. She held on a little longer and squeezed him as she pulled away.

"I'm so excited. Can we get you anything?" Jacqueline asked.

"I'm fine," Joliet answered and looked at Donovan.

"Nothing for me, thanks," he replied.

Jacqueline clapped. "Let's get started." She held her hand out toward the chairs, inviting Joliet and Donovan to sit. She joined them. "I want to thank you for making the time to meet with me Friday evening." She smiled seductively at Donovan. When she turned to Joliet, her smile appeared more cordial. "How's your husband, Joliet?"

"He's much better. Resting his ankle. Thanks for asking."

Jacqueline placed a hand over her heart. "Thank goodness." Moving her hand, she said, "Let's continue. What have you got for me?" Jacqueline clasped her hands together.

Joliet started speaking while Donovan opened the portfolio. "Besides the information you provided, we did a little research and are sure you'll find our offering impressive."

The three of them stood over the conference table as Joliet and Donovan laid out the pictures of decorative options, swatches of linens, floral and menu samples and the information regarding the golf course Jacqueline inquired about in their meeting at Josephina's the other night. Joliet explained the thought behind each choice presented.

"This looks wonderful. I think the brunch and golf tournament will make this a weekend to remember. To be honest, I've been trying to think of a way to take this from a one-night event to a weekend full of activities. It all came to me Friday morning when I recalled that beautiful golf course next to your place. That's one of the reasons I asked for the last-minute meeting. It's a great way to bring more money to the foundation. I figured we could start with the golfing event this year. Next year, I could switch it up and include something on one of those fabulous yachts on the marina near Chandlers. This will be great!"

"It sounds like we're ready to move forward," Donovan nudged.

Jacqueline looked up at him from across the table. A smile teased the corners of her lips. After a moment of overtly washing her eyes over him, she held her hand out. "Looks like we have a deal." They shook. Jacqueline removed her hand from his slowly before turning to shake Joliet's hand.

Joliet discreetly gave Donovan a knowing smile. He knew that Joliet would tease him later about the fact that Jacqueline was obviously sweet on him.

Pulling a contract from her bag, Joliet sat and began reviewing the terms. After finalizing a date, which was in just a few weeks, Jacqueline signed in all the necessary places and they all shook hands again.

"Looks like we're done just in time for my next meeting." Joliet looked at her watch.

Donovan felt his chest tighten. He wondered if they would see Chloe and El on their way out. He needed to see Chloe.

"We'll be in touch." Joliet nodded as they headed out of the conference room.

Donovan's apprehension grew a little more with each step toward the front of the office. The small talk between Jacqueline and his mother droned in the background. Without seeing Chloe, he sensed her. Anticipating her presence, he was deflated when she wasn't already waiting up front.

Jacqueline gave her final greeting and directed her attention to her receptionist. Donovan pushed the door open for his mother to exit and found El standing on the other side. Chloe's scent reached him. He looked past El to find Chloe standing behind her.

She was beautiful. He missed her immediately but remembered he was confused by the distance she'd put between them without explanation in the past few days. He couldn't distinguish the look in her eyes, but thought it best to address their issues in private later.

"Pardon me." El came through the door, mouth pursed in irritation.

"Ms. Chandler." Donovan was polite. He nodded cordially despite her aloof demeanor.

El didn't respond. She continued past him and paused. Donovan turned back to find her and Joliet standing face-to-face. It seemed they were in competition to see whose chin could be held higher. All movement ceased as they stared at each other. Seconds ticked by as if time had morphed into slow motion. Jacqueline continued chatting with her receptionist, oblivious to the tension that filled the air like thick noxious smoke.

Donovan couldn't be concerned about their age-old rivalry. Leaving them to their staring match, he turned to Chloe, using those brief moments to try to read her. Chloe's eyes narrowed at first but she quickly recovered, shifting to a stoic expression.

"Hello, Chloe," Donovan finally said.

"Donovan." She nodded and turned her focus elsewhere.

"Well!" Jacqueline's tone cut through the tension. "You're here!" she proclaimed. "We can go right into the conference room." She started in that direction.

El whipped her head and followed Jacqueline toward the back without saying a single word to Joliet or Donovan.

"Gladly. We're very excited to present our package to you." El's voice sounded as if it were off in the distance to Donovan.

He kept his focus on Chloe. Their eyes connected again, Donovan's held questions but Chloe averted hers and fell in step behind her mother.

"Hello, Mrs. Rivers," Chloe said and smiled. His mother received a warm greeting from Chloe but Donovan didn't.

At least he knew for sure that something was up. He

would no longer be plagued by uncertainty. He walked to the car preoccupied with his discovery, wondering what triggered this change in Chloe. Had he said something? Done something? He couldn't recall. And if he had, why wouldn't she simply tell him? Hadn't they cleared the lines of communication as much as they spoke?

Absently, he opened the door for his mother, rounded the car and drove back to the catering hall. Donovan intended to find out what Chloe's problem was by the end of the night. He needed answers.

Chapter 21

Chloe watched El struggle to maintain her composure when Jacqueline told her that she had decided to go with La Belle Riviere for the gala. Jacqueline wouldn't have sensed it but Chloe knew her mother. Jacqueline went on to explain that she wanted to meet again soon because she was very interested in Chandlers for possible future events. At that point, Chloe didn't believe El was listening. The tightness of her grin was a clear indication that there was no joy behind that facade.

"Thank you so much, Elnora." Jacqueline shook El's hand and turned. "Chloe." She nodded. "And I look forward to working with you in the future."

"You're quite welcome," El said as she clenched her jaw. "Call us whenever you're ready."

"And thank you for the opportunity to present to you," Chloe added.

Jacqueline moved toward the door. "I'll walk you out." El and Chloe followed behind. "Have a wonderful day," Jacqueline said when they reached the door.

"And you do the same." El walked out and moved swiftly toward the car.

Chloe took a deep breath before entering the car. She thought about Donovan and Jacqueline in the restaurant the other night. The memory of Jacqueline's fingers caressing the back of Donovan's hand came to the forefront. Chloe huffed and entered the car.

El slammed her door hard. "I want to know what Joliet did to get this contract. I wouldn't put anything past that woman."

Chloe wondered if Donovan was the apple that fell near his mother's underhanded tree. "Why? Do you suspect Mrs. Rivers did something to sabotage us getting the contract?" She started the car and slowly pulled into traffic.

El looked straight ahead, straightened her posture and settled into her seat.

"Ma. Would Mrs. Rivers do something like that?" Chloe needed to know. Perhaps Donovan earned his tactics honestly. What if his mother put him up to it? Did that family have any integrity?

El still hadn't responded. Chloe wondered why she remained so tight-lipped now. She'd been carrying on about Joliet since forever.

Chloe left her question hanging. It was obvious El didn't feel like talking. This wasn't the first time they had lost a lucrative contract but Joliet wasn't the person they'd lost to either. That made all the difference.

When Chloe thought about it further, she was almost relieved. With all the time she'd been investing into putting together this reception, adding the gala would have made her workload practically unbearable. They still had to run the daily operation as well as the events that had already been booked. Losing that contract could have been a blessing in disguise.

"I don't trust that woman," El finally responded as Chloe maneuvered the car toward the highway. "Never did."

"Why?" Chloe asked. She wanted to know what was between those women. She needed to know, but El went back to her silent stance.

The remainder of their workday carried a stifling weight of defeat. Gone was the normal banter. Heads were down. Work was done. Coworkers hardly spoke.

That same atmosphere followed Chloe home at the end of her day. However, in additional to dealing with the loss and her mother's anger, Chloe was torn. She wanted to cast all thoughts about Donovan aside but couldn't. Regardless of how much distance she'd put between her and Donovan this past weekend, she still longed for him.

Random thoughts and feelings haunted her. She could be driving home and hear the deep timbre of Donovan's voice, whispering in her ear as clearly as if he were right there in the car. Chloe could be walking through the corridors at work and feel Donovan's caress along her cheek or his hand imprinted in the small of her back. Images of her lying in his strong arms showed up behind her eyelids like a live stream.

Chloe tried to shake all these things away but still wanted to be his butterfly. Chloe missed him, fiercely.

Reminding herself of his betrayal, she called on the memory of him sitting in that restaurant with Jacqueline pining over him. The look on her mother's face and the sinking feeling she felt immediately after Jacqueline told them she chose to go with his family's venue was another reminder of why she shouldn't yearn for him.

None of it worked. Her body still craved his touch.

Chloe made it home and headed straight to her backyard in search of solace. She'd created the space to be her sanctuary and right now she needed to be wrapped in some sense of ease.

Chloe stepped out of her shoes, walked along the paved path to the bench amid her garden. She inhaled deeply, taking in the scent of lavender and mint. Closing her eyes, she focused on the soothing sounds of the water gurgling from the fountain, until that was all she could hear. She stayed that way for a moment, breathing evenly.

Chloe felt something soft brush against her leg. Her eyes popped open and she looked down in time to see a beautiful monarch butterfly flurry way. Instantly, Donovan came to mind. Never mind the fact she'd had her gardener plant a host of lavender, daylilies, sage and zinnias to attract the insects. Chloe huffed, wishing she could turn off her feelings with the flick of a switch.

Chloe got up and headed to the kitchen to make a cup of tea. As she turned on the fire, the bell rang. Not feeling up to having company, Chloe sighed and trudged to the living room. She inhaled and exhaled sharply when she saw Donovan outside her door. For a moment she thought about not answering. Donovan's next knock was more persistent. Chloe stood still another moment before opening the door.

The two of them stood there staring at one another. A rush of emotions sailed through Chloe, causing her breath to catch. Seeing his face so close reminded her of how much she missed him. A part of Chloe wanted to wrap her arms around his neck, the other part wanted to slap him for making a fool of her. Right there, she questioned how she could allow herself to fall for him.

"Chloe," Donovan spoke first.

His voice pulled her from the emotional wrestling match. She remembered to be mad. "Yes." Her tone was short.

Donovan's brows furrowed in confusion. "Are you going to invite me in?"

Chloe huffed, stepped aside and let him pass. Closing the door behind her, she headed back to the kitchen to check on her hot water for her tea before returning to her yard. If she was going to have a conversation with Donovan, she needed to be in her sanctuary.

Chloe gestured for him to have a seat. "Can I get you something to drink?"

"I'm fine." Donovan rubbed his chin pensively, before looking over at her. "What's going on, Chloe?"

"You tell me, Donovan." She sat back.

Donovan shrugged, looking clueless. "Did I do something or say something to offend you?"

Chloe sighed and looked away. She wondered if opening up was worth it. Donovan's obliviousness seemed sincere but she refused to be taken for a fool.

"I've been trying to catch up to you all weekend," Donovan continued. "You're not answering my texts or returning my calls and when you do, you're short with me. Is this because I asked you to tell your family about us?"

Was he really oblivious as to why she was angry? Chloe wondered.

"That has nothing to do with it." Chloe swallowed. "Congratulations on winning the contract. Could that have anything to do with your dinner with Jacqueline the other night? Is that why you canceled our plans?" Chloe stood. Her emotions rushed her. She tried to keep them at bay.

Donovan stood as well. "What?"

"I saw you, Donovan." The dam gave in to the pressure of her emotions. Her hands trembled. "My sisters and I were at the restaurant. The two of you were all over each other. I never expected you to be underhanded. Dinner on a Friday night and the contract offer on Monday morning. I guess if I were an attractive man willing to use my sex appeal in unconscionable ways, we could have secured that contract ourselves." She hated losing control. She willed her tears not to spill in front of Donovan. It took all of this for her to realize how much she truly cared for him.

Donovan looked left and right before recognition flashed in his eyes. "What?" His tone was incredulous. "Chloe. No! This is not what you're thinking." Donovan began to explain. "That dinner was business. The only reason I went was because my mother went to the emergency room with my father. She asked me to take the meeting for her."

Chloe didn't know whether or not to believe him.

A contemplative look deepened the lines in his face. With hands planted on his head, Donovan walked a circle around himself. "You think I seduced Jacqueline to win the contract?" Donovan said with creased brows and a finger pointed sharply in her direction.

Chloe folded her arms but didn't speak a word.

"Answer me, Chloe," he demanded, stepping closer.

"Did you?" Chloe's tone wasn't as harsh but she didn't back down.

"You're accusing me of…" Donovan paused and reared back, tilting his head sideways. "You really think I'm capable of that?" He seemed genuinely hurt. Slowly he sat back down in the chair.

Chloe grunted. "Truthfully I don't know, Donovan." Chloe bit back the rest of what she wanted to say. She didn't have enough information to accuse him of taking after his mother. She looked at Donovan, shaking his head. The painful expression in his eyes made her second-guess her position. To avoid acting unreasonably, she decided to cut the conversation short. "I… I don't know. Maybe we should just forget about all this," she said, referring to more than their current squabble. "It's all too much."

"Is that what you want?" he asked.

There was a pleading in Donovan's voice that reached Chloe's heart. She couldn't bring herself to say yes even though she thought that it was best. Even if she was wrong about his intentions with Jacqueline, how could she tell her family about Donovan now? It would be easier to just part ways. She could let this tiff be the catalyst for their demise. Eventually, she'd get over her yearning for his touch, their conversations and the way he referred to her as his butterfly.

"Is. This. What. You. Want." Donovan spoke deliberately as if he'd been speaking to someone who didn't know the language. He stood inches from her.

Chloe couldn't bring herself to look in his face. Sure, she wanted Donovan but she couldn't say it. It would take too much. Wrapping her arms around herself, she nodded only slightly.

Donovan stood in front of her for a moment before backing away. Chloe tried to avoid his eyes as he gradually pulled out his keys, fiddled with them for a moment before stepping back. She didn't move but watched through her periphery as he walked through her home and out her front door. She wanted to stop him from leaving but didn't.

The sound of the door closing startled Chloe. She flinched, held herself tighter and finally let the tears fall.

Chapter 22

Donovan's emotions had surged to a red-hot peak. He didn't want to, but thought it best to leave Chloe's house when he did. Both of them needed to calm down.

Donovan had never been accused of acting without integrity, especially when it came to business. He considered himself a stand-up man. As annoyed as she'd just made him, he couldn't accept this as the end. Proving himself wasn't something he ever felt compelled to do, but somehow he needed Chloe to know that his intentions were never short of noble.

Worst of all, the timing was horrible. Chloe had seen him at that restaurant. Donovan had been careful not to lead Jacqueline on but she'd been so blatant in her flirting that from a distance, one couldn't tell that he wasn't a willing party. Though he understood how his dinner with Jacqueline could be misconstrued, he still couldn't believe that Chloe thought he was capable of being so dastardly.

Donovan would have to be the one to fix this and he was up to the challenge. He wanted Chloe. The time they'd spent together in the past few months only deepened his desire for her. He had never been one to run at a hint of trouble. He'd dug his heels in when he told her that he was no longer interested in keeping their relationship a secret. Donovan had tired of that secret long before.

Giving up now wasn't an option. In order for their relationship to be what he'd envisioned, he needed answers from Chloe and his mother.

Donovan turned left at the next light instead of right and headed toward his parents' home. He was going to get answers tonight. There was no way he'd allow their issues of the past to hinder his plans for the future. If they weren't willing to get on board Team Donovan and Chloe, then they would have to move forward without their blessing. He meant that for Chloe's parents also.

Fifteen minutes later, Donovan pulled into his parents' circular drive. The sun, in the beginning of its stunning descent, cast intense orange and red hues across their meticulous landscape—colors that reinforced Donovan's own mood.

Using his key, he entered their home. "Mom. Dad." He repeated the call, walking through the first floor until someone responded.

"Hey!" his father yelled. "In here."

"Dad?" Donovan followed the sound of his response. William Rivers sat comfortably in the den flipping channels, with his legs propped on an ottoman and a PC on his lap.

"What's happening, son?"

"I need to speak to you and Mom."

"Well, you'd better catch her before she heads out. She's got a meeting tonight with one of those organizations she's involved with." Mr. Rivers craned his neck toward Donovan. "Is everything all right?"

"I just need to talk to the two of you. Ma!" Donovan raced up the steps taking two at a time.

"In here," she called out.

Donovan found her in the master bathroom. Joliet brushed mascara on her lashes. He leaned toward her to kiss her cheek.

"Can you come down? I need to speak with you and Dad. It's important."

Joliet checked her lashes, painted red on her lips and pressed them together. "It will have to be brief, honey, I have a meeting this evening."

"This shouldn't take long at all."

"Okay. I'll be right there."

Back downstairs, Donovan poured a glass of ice tea and paced the perimeter of the kitchen island until he heard his mother descend. He joined them in the family room. Sitting, he looked from one to the other.

"I need to know the history between our family and the Chandlers."

Mr. Rivers raised a brow and looked at Joliet.

"Do we have to do this now?" she asked incredulously.

Donovan stood. "Yes, Mom." He was firm but respectful. "Please." His voice was softer. "It's important."

Joliet sighed. "You really care about this girl."

"I do." Donovan eased back into his chair.

"Well." Joliet tossed her hands up. "What do you want to know?"

"What happened between you and Mrs. Rivers?"

A sigh and a long pause preceded her explanation. "It started back in college," Joliet began.

Chapter 23

"Aunt Ava Rae is in town and wants to do dinner. I know that you usually go to the city with Donovan—"

"I'm not going to the city tonight," Chloe cut Jewel off mid-sentence.

"Oh," Jewel said. "Okay." She spoke slowly. "You still haven't spoken to him, have you?"

"What's there to speak about? I know what I saw and days later they get the contract." Chloe sucked her teeth. "That's not a good look."

The next few moments were filled with dense silence. Chloe knew Jewel was trying to choose her words.

"You're going to just let this whole thing unravel without an attempt at least one civil encounter?"

Chloe blew out an exasperated breath and didn't answer at first. "What about Aunt Ava Rae?" she finally asked, knowing Jewel wouldn't have rescued her from the silence. Chloe didn't really feel like hanging out but couldn't refuse quality time with her aunt. As the mother of four boys, their aunt viewed Chloe, Jewel and Jade as the daughters she'd never had. She was fun, refreshingly honest and full of witty yet solid advice. They adored her. Sometimes El became a little envious.

"She wants to have dinner with us," Jewel said. "She tried to call you."

Chloe moved the phone from her ear and looked at her

call log. She had indeed missed a call from their aunt. "Where are we going?" she said, putting the phone back up to her ear.

"Not Josephina's," Jewel said with a slight snort.

"Jewel!" Chloe didn't think it was funny.

"You two need to talk and stop acting like children," Jewel said matter-of-factly, referring to Chloe and Donovan.

"I told you, there's nothing to talk about."

"I'm forever on your side, sis, but I don't believe Donovan would have seduced Jacqueline or anyone for that matter to close a deal. He's a good guy. That's below his standard. Believe me, she isn't the first beautiful client they've had. I just think the two of you need to sit and have a civil conversation before you just walk away. I love the woman you've become since the two of you have been dating. I don't want to have to say goodbye to her."

Jewels words provoked Chloe's curiosity. "What do you mean, you like the woman I've become?"

"You've changed. You're lighter, perkier. And the smile that slides across your face at the mere mention of Donovan's name makes it seem like someone turned the light on."

"Really?" Chloe hadn't thought about it. Being with Donovan made her happy on the inside and it showed on the outside. She remembered her mother asking what was up with her the day she came to work humming. That's why the past few days without him were so hard. He would have spent at least a few evenings at her house during the week. She missed him so much—especially at night when she lay alone watching TV trying to rid her mind of him. His touch felt like phantom caresses. "I'll see." She wasn't going to commit to anything.

Donovan was probably pretty angry with her. Chloe had accused him of having no integrity and could only imagine how she would feel had someone made those claims against her character. She was torn.

"What time is dinner?" Chloe asked, not wanting to think about the situation anymore.

"Seven. I could pick you up on the way," Jewel offered. "Jade said she'd meet us there because she's going out after."

"I'll be ready."

"Good. See you around six forty-five."

Chloe hung up the phone and sat on the chaise in the sitting area off of her bedroom. Jewel's words stirred in her mind. Chloe hadn't spoken to Donovan since their heated interaction. She'd ignored a few missed calls even though she longed to hear his voice, craved his touch and missed the flutter that erupted in her stomach every time he crossed her threshold.

However, she wasn't totally convinced that he was completely innocent. She just didn't want to be taken for a fool in case it was true and right now she wasn't sure what to believe. Donovan had clearly been upset when he left her home the other day. Since then, she second-guessed what she thought she saw but how else could they explain the contract going to the Riverses immediately after?

Chloe sighed and headed to her walk-in closet. Time was passing and Jewel would soon be at her door. Still wavering, she tried to put the thoughts of the situation between her and Donovan behind her. She had a much bigger issue. Even if Donovan was innocent, after the way El responded to losing the contract to Joliet, how could she ever admit to her mother that she was serious about him?

Maybe she could use their circumstance as a clean break. That way she'd never have to deal with the family drama that was sure to come from their relationship.

The thoughts proved easier than the actions. She could walk away from Donovan now but she didn't really want to. She cared for him and loved that he coaxed parts of her to the forefront—aspects she thought had been buried for years. He made her live again, indulged her passions and forced her to put herself first for a change. It felt great. Even being mad at him hadn't changed that.

Chloe stood at the entrance to her closet but looked off into space, past the clothing that hung there. Huffing, she pulled a black romper from a hanger. Putting it up to her frame, she tilted her head and stared at her reflection in the full-length mirror.

Again Donovan entered her thoughts. They would have been on their way to the city by now, in the car singing along with the radio, laughing and stealing kisses at stoplights. Not tonight. Things had changed so fast.

Chloe freshened up and dressed. The second she pulled her romper in place, her cell phone rang. She told Jewel she'd be down in a few minutes. Chloe finished getting dressed, drew on eyeliner, brushed on mascara and painted a coat of gloss on her lips before heading to the car.

"You look cute," Jewel said when she reached the car. "Let's go. I'm running late and Aunt Ava Rae is already there."

Jewel shaved a cool ten minutes off the drive to the restaurant. By the time they reached their destination, Chloe's right foot was numb from pressing nonexistent brakes on the passenger side of the car. Her hands cramped from holding the bar over the door so tightly. She didn't have to look to know that her knuckles were blanched.

Jade and her aunt were at the bar when she and Jewel went inside. Aunt Ava Rae slid off the bar stool and pulled both of them into a tight embrace.

"How are my girls?"

"Good, Auntie," Chloe said. Seeing her aunt's beautiful face gave her the first genuine smile since she'd seen Donovan with Jacqueline the week before.

"Mom said to tell you to stop trying to steal her daughters," Jewel said, giving her aunt a good laugh as she communicated their ongoing joke.

"Whatever! El is just jealous!"

Ava Rae held her finger up toward the hostess and she led them to a table. The four eased into animated conversation. Jewel's accounts of recent dates kept them laughing and entertained right through their appetizers.

"When you finally find the right one, I'll let you in on a few secrets to keeping things hot, fun and fresh."

"Oh, Auntie!" Jade said. "Spill it. I want to know now."

"These secrets are reserved for 'the one.'" Ava Rae curled her fingers into air quotes when she said, *the one*.

"Tell her what you told me, Auntie." Jewel's excitement at Ava Rae's advice was evident.

Ava Rae looked at her questionably. "Specifically, what do you want me to share with her?"

"The information about the keys to a man's admiration," Jewel said matter-of-factly.

"Oh yes." Ava Rae took the most elegant sip of her wine that Chloe had ever witnessed. Her motions were delicate and mesmerizing.

Chloe nodded, remembering when her aunt had that conversation with her.

"Keys to a man's admiration?" Jade looked puzzled.

"Yes, girl. Listen closely because it sure does work. You see how Uncle Benjamin practically worships the ground she walks on," Jewel added.

"Do I need to take notes?" Jade held up her phone.

"Maybe." Chloe laughed. "It gets intense."

Ava Rae placed her wine glass on the table. "The first key is femininity." Jade's head reared back at Ava Rae's comment. She held a hand up, gesturing for Jade to keep listening. "Men instinctively respond to it. It can be as simple as the arch of your back, a sweet smile, the dip of your shoulder or playful bats of your eyelashes. It's akin to the honey instead of vinegar cliché. Men don't even realize they're being pulled in."

"No way!" Jade's mouth dropped. "You mean act like a damsel in distress."

"No. I mean, act like the lady that you are." Ava Rae looked around the restaurant. The girls craned their necks following her eyes. "I'll show you. Watch this." Ava Rae held up her hand summoning their waiter. "Excuse me," she said, her back rigid. "Can I get some more water please?" Her tone was dry.

"Sure," the waiter said and walked off, not paying much attention.

Jade looked puzzled.

"Keep watching." The manager of the restaurant had been walking around greeting patrons at their tables. Ava Rae winked at Jade. Jewel and Chloe giggled, knowing what was coming.

"Good evening." He bowed slightly. "Are you lovely ladies enjoying your meals?"

"Yes, we are." She dipped one shoulder forward and smiled sweetly. The manager's eyes brightened and his smile spread further across his face. "I have a question." Her voice was lighter than when she spoke to the waiter moments before.

The man floated to her side of the table. "I hope I have an answer."

Did my aunt just giggle? Chloe said to herself and sat back to take in the scene.

"I absolutely love this place but I must say I was a little disappointed during my last visit." She subtly batted her eyes. The way she shifted in her chair reminded Chloe of the easy movement of silk. Ava Rae tilted her head and smiled again. "The service was a little slow. I assumed it was because it was a little crowded but that had never happened before."

"No. We can't have beautiful customers walking away disappointed. I'll tell you what, your drinks and dessert are on the house tonight." The gentleman looked up. "Carlos." He waved another waiter over. "Bring these ladies a bottle of our finest." He paused and looked at the wine glasses on the table and then planted his eyes right back on Ava Rae. "That looks like a Cabernet," he said.

"You're good." She arched her back and lifted her brows, seemingly impressed.

The manager smiled proudly, pleased that he'd fascinated her. "Bring them my favorite Cabernet Sauvignon. You know which one. Also, have the chef prepare a nice dessert sampler for them. Make sure he adds the tart. It's on the house." He turned back to the women. "You'll love it!"

"How sweet of you?" Ava batted her eyes again. The gesture was more pronounced than the moment before.

Taking Ava Rae's hand in his, he rested his other hand on top. "It's my pleasure. Enjoy, ladies." He kissed the back of her hand before leaving the table without paying much attention to the rest of them. It was almost like they weren't even there.

Just as he walked away, the waiter returned with the water she requested. "Thank you," Ava Rae said, void of all the sugary sweetness she'd just laid on the manager.

"You're welcome," the waiter said indifferently before walking away.

When the waiter was out of earshot, Ava Rae sipped her wine and looked at Jade. "See the difference?"

Jade's mouth dropped. The girls burst out laughing.

"The other key is subtlety. There's power in femininity as long as you don't abuse it. You'll have them tripping over themselves to cater to you without even realizing it. Believe me. I've studied it."

"Whoa!" Jade was amazed, but for Chloe, it was a refresher, though she hadn't used it lately.

She thought about applying what she'd learned from her aunt to her relationship with Donovan. The second that thought left her mind, she remembered they didn't have a relationship anymore. A wave of sadness cloaked her. She tried to literally shake it off.

"Now, Chloe." Ava Rae grabbed her attention. "What's up with that Rivers boy?"

Chloe's mouth fell ajar. She recovered quickly and tossed a scathing glare in Jewel's direction. Jewel looked away.

"Never mind how I know." Ava Rae waved off her reaction. "What are you going to do about him?"

"I think we're done."

"Why? Because of your mother?"

"That and other things." Chloe focused on the stem of her glass. "Although I'd love to know what happened between those two."

Ava sat back, allowing the waiter to place the dessert sampler in front of her. "She never told you?"

All three of them shook their heads.

"Do you know?" Chloe cleared her throat, realizing she sounded a little desperate.

Ava nodded, digging a spoon into the enticing tart sitting pretty on the plate full of decadent desserts. The girls watched intently, waiting for a clue to fall from their aunt's mouth. They wondered if she would tell what she knew.

"They used to be the best of friends," Ava Rae started. "Their fallout was painful and ugly."

Chloe, Jewel and Jade passed shocked looks amongst themselves.

"I shouldn't be the one telling you this, but I know my

sister-in-law won't tell you willingly." Ava Rae trained her eyes on Chloe. "And it's obvious that you like this young man so I feel compelled to share what I know." Ava Rae sat back and sighed. "Your mother was dating this guy—a ball player. His name was Gary—Gary Barnes," she recalled. "He was a charmer but arrogant as hell." Ava Rae twisted her lips in disgust. "Yet absolutely gorgeous! To El, he seemed like a sweet, sweet teddy bear. It was their junior year. She and Joliet were roommates and he lived off campus. One night, everyone was supposed to meet at his place for a get-together. El would arrive late because of work. Joliet got there first. By the time the others arrived, Joliet was gone. Gary shared that Joliet came on to him and he had to kick her out. El was furious. They got into a heated argument and Joliet asked to have her room switched."

"Oh my goodness!" Chloe said. Concern spread across their faces.

"After that, Joliet beat El out of a job at a place where they interned together. El was convinced Joliet had somehow sabotaged her opportunity. When she married your father, El did everything to keep Joliet away from my brother even though we had all been friends for many years—growing up together in the same neighborhood. Their friendship spiraled into the nasty competitive rivalry it is today."

"Do you still speak to Mrs. Rivers, Auntie?" Chloe asked.

Ava Rae shrugged. "Occasionally, but she and I weren't the close ones as youngsters. She was part of Bobby Dale's crew of friends. I never got involved in their stuff."

Wow! Between losing the contract and this history, Chloe thought she'd never be able to bring Donovan home.

Chapter 24

We need to talk. Donovan tapped out another text. Chloe had been ignoring most of them. When she did respond, her answer was concise. I'm busy.

Donovan needed to speak with her about her accusations and share the information that he'd learned from his mother. It seemed like one big misunderstanding compounded by hurt feelings. He was convinced that sharing what he'd learned with Chloe could make a difference.

Donovan also felt a need to clear the air. He didn't want the end of what seemed like the start of a promising relationship to be so abrupt. They should be able to talk this out and make a decision on whether or not to move forward without arguing. Even if they decided to part ways, he needed it to be a civil parting. His thinking was more rational now that he'd had time to calm down and think. Despite how distraught he felt when he left her house the other evening, he missed her terribly.

Putting his cell phone down, Donovan sat in the driver's seat and stared into the nothingness. Though he'd left a while ago, he hadn't pulled out of his parents' driveway.

He still hadn't processed the information his mother shared with him. His heart lurched even now as he recalled the tears streaming down her face. It seemed that going through the details freshened the hurt and anger she'd felt all those years before. He was almost sorry he'd asked her to tell him what happened.

Mr. Rivers comforted Joliet before she went back upstairs to freshen up her makeup. When she finally did leave, her mood had been somber. Donovan hoped getting together with her fellow organizational members would lift her spirits.

Donovan turned the key in the ignition and slowly pulled out. He knew Chloe was just being stubborn by not responding to his texts. He headed toward her house to make another attempt to communicate with her.

Along the way, he thought about the fact that, had this been a normal Friday evening, they would have been in Manhattan. Donovan would be swaying under the sound of Chloe's beautiful voice as she sang the club into a trance. Then she'd come down off the stage and run right into his arms—arms that ached to hold her—arms that missed the feel of her between them at night as they curled into one another in bed.

Instinctively, Donovan frowned. He didn't like feeling torn. Being upset by her accusations and aloofness didn't change the fact that he still wanted her. Her saving grace was the fact Donovan could understand her perspective. Had he seen her in that restaurant with another man crawling over her, he would have been furious.

Donovan had wanted Chloe for years but kept his distance. Having her in his arms was next level. He hadn't imagined enjoying her company so much. He hadn't known she was fun and talented and sensual and adventurous and uninhibited in bed.

Donovan closed his eyes, relishing the memory of how their bodies mingled so perfectly as if they were made to fit one another. He opened his eyes and grunted. Had this been some other woman, he would have decidedly walked away days ago and never looked back. With Chloe, he simply couldn't.

When Donovan pulled up in front of her house, he spotted her car. Halfway up the walkway, he noticed there weren't any lights on except the dim living room light that she left on when she wasn't at home. He stopped walking, peered at the window, climbed the front steps, knocked and rang the bell several times. She wasn't there. Already he sensed that it was empty. Chloe's presence filled the space with energy.

At first, Donovan wondered if she'd gone into Manhattan without him but doubted it. Being upset with him, she probably wouldn't venture to a place they frequented together.

Donovan trudged back to his car, slightly annoyed. Despite how things had turned out between them, he wanted to get this conversation over with. If he had to move on without her, he would. Either way, he needed to know what the future held. He needed to have this conversation with Chloe soon.

Donovan got his brother Dayton on the phone.

"What's up, man?" Dayton's voice was cheerful.

"Not much. Are you busy? Want to hit The Reserve?" Donovan mentioned Chris Chandler's new wine and jazz bar, almost hoping he'd run into Chloe. If not, it was the perfect setting for a leisurely night out with his brother.

"Sure. I was just hanging out here at the house."

"Good. I'm glad I caught you before you found something or someone to get into. Ha!"

"You're right!" Dayton laughed right along with Donovan. "What time?"

Donovan looked at his watch. "I'm heading over there now."

"Cool. See you there!" Dayton said.

Donovan drove through the starry night until he reached

the half-mile stretch where restaurants lined the sidewalk alongside coffee houses, a Pilates studio, a painting bar and trendy high-end boutiques. The Reserve was nestled right in the center of the block. He circled a few times before finally finding a parking spot around the corner.

Inside, the elegant establishment boasted a romantic yet jazzy theme. The monochromatic décor reflected varying shades of gray from the high-backed leather seating to the silk drapes and contemporary lighting fixtures. Black-and-white pictures of jazz greats hung on three walls. The fourth wall, behind the bar, held countless wine bottles behind impeccably clear glass casings.

Donovan knew that Chris had opened the wine bar with friends but didn't doubt that a woman had lots to do with the decor. He wondered if Chloe had input.

The place was bustling. Waitresses hastened to and from tables dressed in all black. Donovan recognized the melody of one of Miles Davis's songs being played by the three-piece band.

A waif-thin redhead greeted him with a smile as he stepped further inside. "Good evening."

"Evening." Donovan nodded. "I'm waiting for one person."

"Will it be just the two of you?"

"Yes."

"Wonderful. Just let me know when your other party arrives. I should be able to seat you fairly soon."

"Thanks." Donovan stepped just outside the restaurant, taking in the business of the area as he waited for his brother.

Dayton arrived soon enough and they were seated, placed orders for a few appetizers and requested a bottle of The Reserve's choice red wine.

After several moments of small talk, Donovan began to feel better. Glad that he decided to hang out with his brother instead of mulling over his situation with Chloe, he bobbed to the music.

"You still pull out your sax or trumpet every now and then?" Dayton asked, swirling the wine the waitress just poured into a glass. He sniffed, sipped and nodded his approval before she filled his glass halfway.

"Wow! It's been a long time. I need to dust it off and try it out. What about you?"

"I haven't touched that sax in years." Dayton laughed. "If it wasn't such great quality, it probably would have rusted by now," he joked. Another sip. "So what's up with you and Chloe? I figured that you'd have her over for dinner after your big announcement."

Donovan pulled his lips in and took a breath. "Yeah. About that."

Concern creased Dayton's forehead. "What happened?"

Donovan shared the events of the past week, paying attention to the surprised look on his brother's face. Normally he would have spoken to him about something like this by now but Donovan hadn't felt up to talking about it with anyone.

"Wow. I would be upset about the accusation too but like you said, I can see how she could think that. The history between our parents doesn't help either. Man!" Dayton shook his head. "What are you going to do?"

"We'll talk." Donovan sounded more confident than he felt.

"You really care about this girl, huh?"

"I'm surprised by it, myself," Donovan admitted. "Initially, I figured Puerto Rico would just be a little fun—two consenting adults sharing in good times and then going our separate ways. We came back home and kept rolling with it until I realized I didn't want it to end and she didn't either."

"Well then, you're doing the right thing. Talk to her." Dayton sat back, allowing the waitress to put the steaming plate with one of their appetizers on the table. "I knew she meant a lot to you when you told the family. That's not something we normally do."

"I know." Donovan chuckled. "Somehow, she got past my defenses. Chloe's a solid woman. I can see having a real future with her."

"Whoa!" Dayton put his drink down and held his hands up and crossed them like a T. "Time out! Are you talking…like marriage?" He leaned closer to Donovan as if it were possible for him to miss his response in the small space between them.

"Yeah." Donovan nodded. "Like, I could see myself marrying her. At least I saw it until this past week."

"Wow." Dayton blinked and took a long sip. "Sounds like she's worth the effort. Try to make it right, big brother."

Donovan intended on doing just that. He just needed to figure out how.

Chapter 25

Chloe had a ball with her aunt and sisters. After dinner, they went to a lounge, danced, drank more wine. She actually got on the microphone during karaoke. Her aunt was blown away.

"Chloe! I didn't know you could sing like that." Ava Rae held her hand against her heart. "That was beautiful." Chloe blushed.

The next morning, they included El and they all went to breakfast and perused their favorite boutiques for some shopping. It had been so long since Chloe had an outing like this that she forgot how much fun it was to hang with the girls. They shopped until they worked up a second appetite. On their way to a restaurant they'd spotted earlier, Ava Rae spied a stunning handbag in the window of one of the shops.

Halting in front of the store, Ava Rae said, "Would you look at that?"

"Look at what?" El asked.

"That bag." Ava Rae pointed with one hand and struggled to hold her floppy hat with the other. The shopping bags she held fell against her shoulder. "I have to check it out," she said, already making her way to the entrance of the store.

"Ava! I'm hungry." El nearly whined.

"Go ahead and get the table. I'll be right behind you."

Chloe, her mother and sisters laughed. Their aunt was a self-proclaimed professional shopper. There was no getting her out of that store.

"Chloe, go with her so she doesn't get lost. We'll get a table. I hope the wait isn't too long," El said.

Laughing, Chloe nodded. "Okay, Mom."

"I'll go, too," Jewel said.

"No!" Chloe and El said at the same time. Jewel was as bad as her aunt when it came to shopping.

"We'll end up losing both of you. Come with me," El instructed.

"Ha! Am I that bad?" Jewel asked.

El, Chloe and Jade looked at each other and all at once they looked at Jewel.

Jewel shrugged. "I guess so." Jewel put her head down bashfully. "Let's go eat?" They laughed some more.

Chloe went after her aunt in the store while the others headed to the bistro.

"Isn't this one lovely?" Ava Rae held up another bag, admiring it.

"That is nice, Auntie." Chloe had to admit the handbag was just as stunning, if not more so, than the one in the window.

Chloe picked up a dress and looked it over while her aunt debated.

"I'll get this one." Ava Rae finally decided. By the time Chloe turned around, her aunt was already heading to the register. The clerk packaged her purchase and handed it to her over the counter with a big smile. "Okay. Let's go to that store on the corner before going to the restaurant."

Chloe shook her head and laughed but obliged. Ava Rae made a few more purchases and gifted Chloe with a dress for her patience.

As they headed out of that second store, Chloe noticed a car sitting at the light that resembled Donovan's. Narrowing her focus, she peered into the driver's side. The light changed and the driver looked both ways before stepping on the gas. Gliding by, he twisted his head in Chloe's direction. She and Donovan locked eyes as she walked. A jolt shot through her but she kept in step with her aunt, trying not to alert her.

Donovan waved. With a half smile and heavy sigh, she waved back. Her aunt seemed oblivious to the entire interaction. Trying to pry her heart away from him was much easier when she didn't have to see his face.

Confusion flooded her brain. She wanted to be done with him, yet missed him more than she could ever remember missing anyone. Finally, she looked away and Donovan picked up his speed in response to the car honking behind him.

Aunt Ava Rae continued speaking, still seemingly unaware that Chloe hadn't been paying attention.

Chloe remembered her words from the night before at dinner. "I know you are a woman now and I would recommend you follow your heart but know that bringing Donovan home would practically kill your mother." She'd laughed after she'd said that but Chloe couldn't seem to find any humor in her words.

For the remainder of her afternoon, Chloe fought off thoughts of how much she missed Donovan. What good would any of that do if she could never seriously consider being with him? Then she thought, was any of this fair to her? What about what she wanted? But what about the sacrifice?

She was right back where she'd started and she was still unsure about Donovan's intentions when it came to Jacqueline. She wanted to give him the benefit of the doubt but didn't want her feelings for him to make a fool of her.

Chloe tried her best to engage with her family. She enjoyed their outing but remained distracted well into the evening.

At home, she sunk into a hot tub bubbling with lavender-scented foam and sipped one more Pinot Noir. Chloe thought it would ease her body and mind but suspected that she'd thwarted those efforts with too much wine throughout the day. Her sleep was restless.

The sound of the doorbell reverberated in Chloe's head as if it were inside of her brain. She pried her eyes open one by one. The sunlight assailed them. Squeezing her eyes shut, she groaned and put her pillow over her head. She drank too much wine the past two days hanging out with her aunt, mother and sisters. It was much better than sulking and fighting with her urges for Donovan alone.

There was that sound again. Chloe moved the pillow and looked at the clock. It wasn't even eight in the morning on a Sunday. Who could this have been?

Suddenly she jumped up. It was probably El. Her mother had been known to show up unexpected at the brink of dawn. Chloe trudged to her window and looked out. Donovan's car sat at the curb.

She froze for a moment and then sighed. Chloe wasn't ready to deal with him even though she'd held back a strong hankering to call his cell phone late last night and invite him over for a nightcap. The wine had given her relationship amnesia. She'd forgotten that they weren't on good terms—or on any terms for that matter. Or did she? The wine could have been a great excuse.

Chloe laughed at herself as she grabbed a robe and headed for the door.

"Who is it?" she said as if she didn't know.

"Donovan."

Chloe didn't expect the rich deep timbre of Donovan's voice to reach through the door and embrace her, provoking a gang of butterflies into flight. He'd done just that with one word. Bracing herself, Chloe put her hand on the doorknob and paused to gather her nerves before easing it open.

"This is unexpected." Pulling her robe tighter, she stepped back to allow him in.

"Good morning." Donovan stared at her.

After a while, she looked away. "What brings you here so early?"

"I figured it was the best way to catch you." He held up a tray with two cups of coffee. She tilted her head toward the kitchen and he followed her. "We need to talk."

Chloe hoped her sigh didn't make her seem rude. She just wasn't ready for this—especially this early while a dull thump repeated at her temple. It was the direct result of too much wine and not enough sleep. "What better time than the present?" Her tone came across more sarcastic than she intended. "I'm sorry."

"It's not a problem." Donovan sat and handed one of the cups to Chloe as she joined him at the table.

Chloe felt a charge as their hands touched. She averted her eyes, not wanting to see if Donovan sensed it. This was hard. Chloe sniffed, delighting in the strong aroma of the coffee and hazelnut creamer. It was her favorite.

"I need you to know that I didn't do anything unscrupulous to get that contract."

Forget the small talk. Donovan was getting right to the point, Chloe thought.

"Jacqueline called that meeting at the last minute. She was really interested in the golf course next to us and wanted to know if we could work with the owner and present her with some kind of package deal. She saw it when she visited and decided to add a golf tournament the Saturday after the gala. She's also interested in having her gala at Chandlers next year and offering some kind of sailing event or renting one of those yachts by the marina."

Donovan took a breath. "Your accusations angered me but I felt compelled to make sure you understood the truth. I thought it would be best for both of us to calm down so we could speak civilly. I still wonder how you could think I would do something like that. I thought you knew me well enough."

Chloe avoided his eyes. Finally looking up, she was taken by his gorgeous brown orbs. "I'm sorry to have insulted you but I didn't know what to think. I still don't know what to think." Her apology was sincere but she knew that was all she could offer him. She'd convinced herself that a relationship was no longer possible. She was willing to at least be friends and she expressed that.

"I'm sorry, too, but I also need you to know that I'm not interested in being friends with you."

Offended, she glared at him. "What?" She wondered if she'd heard him right. Again she was torn; she thought it best to part ways now, too, but hadn't expected him to be so brazen about it.

"I want to be more than your friend. What we had…" Donovan pointed between them "…I want it back—and more."

A sigh of relief lifted Chloe's chest.

"Donovan…" she started.

Donovan held his hand up, halting her words. "We're grown—too grown for games." Donovan slid off the stool he occupied and walked around the island to where Chloe sat. "I had a lot of time to think this past week. I even told my family about you."

Chloe gasped. Her mouth opened and shut several times but her words wouldn't find their way past her lips. There were too many thoughts to sift through in that moment. She wanted to know how they responded to his news but then again she didn't. She imagined El fainting if she ever told her such a thing.

"Donovan... I—" It hurt to complete her sentence. "I can't." *I need more time* would have sounded better. It would have been truer—offered more of a possibility, but the definitive response came out instead. Chloe couldn't take it back now.

As she dithered, Donovan closed the distance between them. In the next instant, she felt his lips on hers. Her first inclination was to resist but his lips on hers felt like the warmth of home. They belonged there.

Her body disobeyed her intent, leaning into his. Her hands found their way around the back of his neck. Greed surged inside of her, compelling her to want much more. A sudden rush of heat engulfed her, sending white-hot signals throughout her body, pebbling her nipples. Then it was over. It took a moment for Chloe to recover. She sat there, panting, eyes closed, lips swollen, her body craving more.

"You can. You'll see that I'm right," Donovan whispered against her ear. "You just need a little time. Just a little." Kissing her temple, Donovan pivoted, picked up his coffee cup and headed for the door.

Chloe never made it out of her chair. Yes, they were grown. Yes, she wanted Donovan. That was obvious but was he worth the rift that it would cause between her and her mother?

Chapter 26

The kiss was a test. Donovan had to know for sure that Chloe wanted to be with him. Was moving forward even possible? It took every ounce of will to pull away from Chloe. He wanted to sweep her off her feet, carry her to the bed and make love to her for the rest of the day. Donovan wondered if he was successful in showing Chloe that she still wanted him as much as he wanted her.

The feel and thoughts of that kiss stayed with him through the day, night and into the next morning. Donovan hummed to the music as he drove to work Monday. He was on his way back to Chloe.

"Sweetie."

Donovan looked up to capture the beautiful, polished sight of his mother entering his office. She was stunning in her gray skirt suit despite the fact her usually cheerful demeanor was gone. It had been since the other night when she shared her story.

"Jacqueline has been called out of the country." Joliet sat on the edge of Donovan's desk. "She needs to move the date of the gala up several weeks." Donovan's eyes widened. "I know," his mother said, knowingly. "Apparently the trip is unavoidable. She has to reshoot scenes from a movie currently in production. That gives us even less time. I spoke with Jim over at the country club and he can do the Saturday after next. We're clear for the night before. Jacqueline has asked for a meeting later this evening so we could go over all of the logistics and see how much this change would cost her."

"We have two weeks to put this thing together?" Donovan slapped the desk.

Joliet huffed. "Yep. And we need to make this work. The following week, Jacqueline is off to Dubai for a month to reshoot the film and then Wales for a few weeks after that on a deal she couldn't refuse. She's been reaching out to all of her contacts to see who can still make the gala. Her team is also working on a new list to send invitations. She's confident that she can still meet the guarantee and fill the room. As she said, 'she's got plenty of friends.'"

Instinctively Donovan looked at his watch. He knew the luxury of time would evade him over these next two weeks. "I'll review the budget now and see how moving the date will impact us."

"Thanks. Once we have that, let's call a meeting to go over everything with the staff."

"No problem, Mom." Donovan opened the Excel file on his computer. "I'll send this over to you as soon as I rework the numbers."

"Thanks." Joliet slid off the desk and headed toward the door.

"Ma."

She turned slowly. "Yes, dear."

"Are you okay?"

"I'm fine, honey. Just fine."

Donovan knew otherwise. He assumed that having his mother rehash that story of her past made her think about her ruined friendship with El. Maybe it could somehow be restored, he thought. That would certainly make life easier for Chloe and him. At some point, he needed to talk to Chloe about what his mother shared. Right now, he needed to brace himself for another close encounter with Jacqueline.

With all the meetings, schedule rearranging, maneuvering budgets and supply ordering, the day went by in a blur of busyness.

Joliet asked Jacqueline if she wouldn't mind meeting them at the venue as opposed to the restaurant she'd requested. Donovan was relieved she obliged. He didn't need another spotting with him and Jacqueline. He was thankful that last one didn't end up on the entertainment pages of any local publications. They loved a good scandal and Jacqueline's behavior was definitely scandal-worthy. He could see the headlines. "Does Jacqueline Bosley Have a New Beau?" above a picture of her laughing in that carefree way with her head thrown back.

Donovan was enveloped in tasks right up until the moment their celebrity client walked through the door. Joliet came to get him and he followed her to the conference room. He figured Jacqueline would tame her flirting with Joliet around but his mother's presence didn't seem to make a difference.

"Oh." Jacqueline purred when Donovan walked through the door, folders in hand.

"Good evening, Ms. Bosley," Donovan said with an outstretched hand.

"Are you kidding me?" Jacqueline swatted his hand and pressed her body against his in a sensual hug. "It's great seeing you again." She air-kissed both sides of his face. "I thought I told you to call me Jackie," she chided as she pulled away.

Behind her, Joliet raised one brow before pulling out a chair and inviting them to join her at the conference table.

"Whew." Jacqueline fanned herself. "Is it hot in here or is it just me?" She released a hearty laugh.

Joliet and Donovan looked at her and each other. "I'm fine," Joliet noted.

"I'm fine, too. I'll turn on the AC." Donovan went to the thermostat and within seconds the sound of whirring air expanded in the room.

"Ah! There we go." Jacqueline sounded relieved. "Maybe it was that hug." She turned to Joliet. "How do you keep women off of him? Tall, dark and handsome is a boring cliché when you're describing that son of yours." She flashed a seductive smile in Donovan's direction.

He smiled cordially. "Thanks, Ms. Bos..." She tossed him a playfully scolding glare, prompting him to change how he addressed her. "Thanks, Jackie," he said pointedly.

"You're welcome. So." Jacqueline clamped her hands together. "What do you have for me?"

Joliet took over explaining the outcome of her meeting with the owners of the country club. "So the biggest change here is going to be the cost since we have to put a rush on a few orders to be prepared." Donovan distributed his budget sheet. "We've made the necessary adjustments to staffing, food and contacted our vendors for the centerpieces and requests you made for the décor. Things should fall right into place. As long as you're okay with the revised pricing, we can move forward. Next, I'd like for you to take a look at the menu to make sure you don't require any changes there."

Jacqueline reviewed each document that was placed before her carefully, inquiring about a few items and listening to the responses intently.

"Is this a new cake vendor?"

"Yes," Joliet replied. "Unfortunately, the initial vendor was unable to squeeze in another order for that weekend. She's terribly sorry and quite upset that she won't get to make your cake. She admires your work and was ecstatic about baking for you."

"Would it be possible for our team to sample new vendors' goods? I don't need any additional surprises at this point."

"Absolutely," Joliet encouraged. "I'm sure we can get something set up for tomorrow. I know you're leaving town the day after."

"Thanks, Joliet."

They reviewed a few more documents before Donovan presented Jacqueline with her revised contract. "So if you'll just sign here." He pointed. "And here, we will be all set."

"Anything for you, Donovan."

The way Jacqueline scrutinized him helped him understand what women meant when they said men made them feel like pieces of meat. Jacqueline could have licked him clean right there in their conference room.

"Oh. One last thing," Jacqueline said. "Joliet, would you mind looking over my new guest list? I've added a few more people whom I think it would be good to have them experience what my galas are like." She handed Joliet a spreadsheet. "Also, I'm sure you're used to this, but there will be plenty of press here that night. Several editors and television producers have confirmed their attendance. I'll need a room set aside for the interviews with the press."

"No problem," Joliet said. "We can set them up in our best bridal suite. The space is conducive to that sort of thing."

"Wonderful!" Jacqueline took out her pen and signed her name in all the designated areas with a flair Donovan had never witnessed. Donovan wondered if all of her mannerisms were exaggerated and if it was authentic. "That copy of the guest list is yours. Let me know if you have any questions regarding any of those names."

Joliet nodded. The three of them stood and shook hands. Together, she and Donovan walked Jacqueline to the door.

Chapter 27

El busted into Chloe's office and tossed an envelope on her desk. Huffing, she paced back and forth. "Look at that. Can you believe it?"

Chloe picked up the envelope curiously—almost not wanting to open it. "What is it?" She looked up at El.

"An invitation."

"To what?" This was like pulling molars. "Mom. What's this about?" Without waiting for an answer, Chloe shook her head and pulled the contents out. The paper was beautiful and made of linen. As Chloe read the script lettering, her eyes stretched wider. "Jacqueline's inviting us to her foundation's gala."

"Yes! It's a personal invitation for the Chandler family to join her as special guests. I don't trust this at all! I'm sure Joliet has something to do with this."

"Ma!" Just as Chloe attempted to calm her down, her cell phone rang. It was her father. "Hey, Dad."

"How's your day, sweetheart?"

Before answering, Chloe looked up at El standing stiffly with her arms crossed. "Just fine." She wondered if her father could sense her sarcasm.

"Good. Is your mom there? I've been trying to call her and she's not answering."

"She's right here in my office."

When they turned back to head to their offices, Donovan looked down at the list in Joliet's hands.

"May I?" he asked, reaching for the list.

"Oh. Sure, honey. When we were on the phone earlier, she mentioned this. She said she wanted to make sure that anyone who was anyone at all got invited to her gala."

Donovan's eyes perused the list, stopping at one name that he was sure to consider a no-show. If they actually came, having them in the same room with Jacqueline for hours could prove challenging.

"Put me on speaker." Chloe did. "Honey." Bobby Dale called out to El.

"Bobby! Can you believe that woman invited us to her gala? This has got to be some tricky business."

"Sweetie. Slow down. What woman…the actress?"

"Yes. The actress," El repeated. "That Joliet is up to something. She probably just wants to rub their win in our faces. I'm not going."

"Now slow down, honey. You don't want to act like that. It's not Joliet's event. The invitation came from Jacqueline, right? It's pretty high profile. Maybe you should consider it. Isn't Chloe working on raising Chandlers' visibility? Your presence at the gala could help."

"Yes!" Chloe got an idea. "And maybe we could invite Jacqueline to our reception. That would be a good look for us, too. We should go. She's considering having her gala at our place next year anyway. This could serve as research."

El straightened her back and stared at Chloe. "Who told you that?"

Chloe realized her mistake. She couldn't possibly say she got the information from Donovan. El would accuse her of fraternizing with the enemy. "Look." Chloe pointed to the invitation. "She's doing a golf challenge at the Beckingham—the country club next to the Riverses' place. That's why she chose their location. I heard she wants to do a sailing or yacht event next year and she'd like to work with Chandlers for that."

El narrowed her eyes at Chloe and then looked away. Chloe could tell she was thinking about everything she just said.

"See, honey?" Bobby Dale's voice came through Chloe's cell phone. "It's not a conspiracy. It's business. You should certainly go."

El lifted her chin and cleared her throat. She tugged

on the bottom of her suit jacket. "All right. I'll go. I need to go shopping."

Bobby Dale's rich, deep laugh barreled through the receiver and filled Chloe's office. Chloe held hers behind a small smile. El didn't laugh at all. In fact, she looked appalled by the fact that Bobby Dale was still cracking up. She turned on her heels and left. When she cleared the doorway, Chloe burst out laughing.

"She stormed off, didn't she?" Bobby Dale assumed aloud, his laughter decreasing to a chuckle.

"She sure did," Chloe confirmed.

"This is going to be some night," Bobby Dale said. "Joliet Rivers, Jacqueline Bosley and your mom in one room. Woo!" He started laughing all over again. Chloe joined him. "Let me get off this phone and call your mother. I think I'm going to need to calm her down."

"Okay. Bye, Dad. Love you."

"Love you, too, sweetheart."

Chloe knew what to expect for El at this event. What she didn't know was how to deal with it herself. Donovan's surprise visit and knee-buckling kiss left her dazed. Memories of his lips on hers taunted her day and night. How was she to deal with all of them in the same room for hours?

Chloe propped her elbows on her desk and rested her head in her hands. Her sight fell on the invitation and that's when she noticed the date. She sat back abruptly. Instead of having two months to prepare their minds for this encounter, they only had two weeks. In addition to that, the gala was the day after the Chandlers' reception.

Chloe groaned and shook her head and then wondered if Donovan knew about this. As much as she intended to avoid Donovan, she wanted to know. Chloe dialed Donovan's number for the first time in over a week.

"What a nice surprise." As always, Donovan's voice aroused her senses.

"Hello, Donovan."

"Hello, Chloe. What can I do for you?"

"I just received an invitation from Jacqueline Bosley to attend her foundation's gala."

"That was quick."

Chloe reared back. "You knew about this?"

"I just found out yesterday when she revised the contract because she needed to change the date. She revamped her guest list and left a copy with us."

"I see. So this was her all her idea," Chloe said, referring to Jacqueline.

"Yep."

"Okay."

No one spoke for moments. The awkward silence made Chloe tense. It felt odd because the conversation had always flowed so easily between them.

"I hope you can make it," Donovan finally said.

"Thanks." Chloe didn't know what else to say to that.

"Are you busy this evening?"

"No." Chloe punched the air. She hadn't meant to answer so quickly. "Why?"

"Well, there's something important I think we need to discuss. My hope is that it will help us move forward. I'm serious about us but just don't want to push you. We can meet at Sandy's by the Shore. I won't keep you out long."

Chloe took in a long deep breath. "What time?"

"Right after work. Let's say…five thirty."

"See you there." Chloe ended the call, wondering what Donovan had to say.

Instead of waiting to the end of her day, she headed home early and freshened up before meeting with Donovan.

Chloe arrived at the restaurant right on time to find Donovan already seated at the bar. Sliding off the bar stool, he greeted Chloe with a kiss. Donovan guided her by the elbow to the hostess and they were seated.

Chloe blushed under the scrutiny of Donovan's gaze. She felt like a prized artifact in a museum. They engaged in small talk over drinks and appetizers. It almost felt the way it used to be between them. Not wanting to tease herself, Chloe decided to get to the reason they got together.

"What's the important information you had to share with me?"

Donovan took a breath, sipped wine and sat back. "I spoke to my mother."

Chloe shifted in her seat. "And."

"She told me what happened between her and your mother."

Chloe held her tongue. She wanted to hear their version.

Donovan ran his finger around the rim of his glass. "I almost felt bad for bringing it up."

Chloe tilted her head. "Why?" Tilting her head, she gave him her complete attention.

"She cried."

"She cried?" Chloe's brows furrowed. Based on what Chloe had learned about the situation, that didn't make sense. "Why would she cry?"

"It hurt that Mrs. Chandler hadn't believed her, but she knew it was that bastard Gary's fault."

"Wait. What did she tell you?"

Donovan took a breath. "Your mother's ex tried to brutally force himself on my mother. She managed to get away before he'd done any real damage, but before she could tell anyone, he'd convinced your mom and all of their friends that my mother had come on to him, betraying your mom. Then he stalked her daily, threatening to do her harm if she said anything to anyone. The stalking really messed her up for a while. It took years for her to finally come out of her shell."

Chloe was practically in tears. With her hand on her heart, she asked, "Did she ever get to tell my mother what happened?"

"No. They never became friends again after that. She told us the story last Friday evening." Donovan sat back and took a breath as if telling the story lifted weight from his chest.

"What about the guy? Did anything ever happen to him?" Chloe asked.

"He went on to play pro basketball but had to stop because of an injury. He also worked as a sports commentator and a coach at a college in New Jersey for a while. Other than that, no one has seen him for years. My dad and I both wish we could find him." For an instant, Donovan's eyes turned menacing.

"That's horrible." Chloe couldn't believe what she heard. If Donovan's story was true, El was mad at Joliet for no good reason. Not to mention this situation ruined a friendship that probably would have lasted for years. "That bastard probably did the same thing to other women, too." Chloe's brows were furrowed. She shook her head. "Why tell me this now?" Chloe asked after a few silent moments. She wanted to ask about the job opportunities that El thought Joliet sabotaged but she didn't. Instead, she told Donovan what she'd learned from her aunt about the situation.

Donovan pushed one of the plates aside and leaned across the table toward Chloe. "If we get them together, just to talk, maybe they could find their way past this so we could be together. I know how much your family means to you and I don't want you to have to choose between them and me, but I'm not willing to let you go so easily."

Chloe let the tears fall. It wasn't for Joliet although she felt for her. These tears were brought on by the effort Donovan put into trying to make things work between them. There was possibly a chance for them to be together. Maybe she should fight for Donovan as hard as he was fighting for her.

Chapter 28

Chloe couldn't believe she'd agreed to this. Frantically, she ran around the first floor of her home, trying to get things in order for the dinner that she and Donovan planned with their mothers. Chloe hadn't told El that Joliet would be there and had no idea how she was going to react.

Looking at her watch, she drew in a sharp breath taking in the delectable scent of the lemon pound cake wafting through the house. Her grandmother Mary Kate had taught her how to make it and eventually she'd mastered the recipe so well that her grandma stopped making it altogether. Now it was Chloe's assignment for all major occasions and family gatherings. It was also El's favorite cake.

"Check the cake," she yelled to Jade and Jewel as she made her way from the dining room to the kitchen.

"Okay!" Jade yelled back, mocking her. She could hear both sisters snickering.

Chloe appeared in the entrance of the kitchen, halted and planted her hands on her hips, catching the girls mid-laugh. She stood there long enough to see them mocking her in high voices the way annoying little sisters would. She refused to laugh, trying her best to look angry. She stayed that way for a few moments until they finally noticed her. When they did, the three of them burst out laughing.

"Sorry, sis, but you need to relax. I feel like I'm in the

kitchen with Mommy with you barking orders like that. Check the cake! Turn the fire down! Stir the vegetables!" Jewel fell out laughing again.

"I know, right?" Jade joined in.

Sighing, Chloe dropped her shoulder. "I'm sorry," she whined.

Jade walked over and threw her arms around Chloe. "We're just teasing. We understand. I would certainly be a wreck if it were me."

"No apologies needed, Sissy." Jewel walked over with her cell phone in her hand and kissed Chloe on the cheek. She looked at the phone. "We don't have much time. Let's get this table set up." Jewel started back toward the stove. "I sure wish I could stick around and see the look on Mom's face when Joliet walks in the door."

"Me, too. I could really use your support." Chloe grabbed a decorative bowl filled with mixed greens, pecans and fresh strawberries. Sliced avocadoes formed a circle in the center.

Jewel pouted. "I know but this show has been sold out for months. I can't forfeit my tickets now. I wish I had known before you made the plans, I would have told you to do it another day so I could watch." Jewel followed Chloe into the formal dining room carrying a dish of the roasted vegetables on a tray made of fine china.

"Yeah, sis. Me, too," Jade said, making room on the table for the dishes her sisters carried.

Jewel looked at Jade and twisted her lips. "You could be here. You just don't want to." She put her tray down, waved off Jade and sauntered back toward the kitchen.

"You know I hate conflict," Jade said, following behind Jewel.

"I'll be fine," Chloe assured them. They continued back and forth until all of the food was out. With fine linens, a tall centerpiece with a spray of seasonal flowers and the formal setting, the table looked fit for the cover of *Gourmet* magazine.

"I'm going to call you the second I get out of the theater. I want to hear every detail. I need to make sure good old El is still standing. Ha!" Jewel untied the apron from her waist.

"You're bad." Jade snickered, removing her apron as well.

Chloe's phone dinged. The text from Donovan read, Are you okay?

I'm doing okay for now, Chloe replied.

Jewel grabbed her bag. "Call you later, sis." She wrapped her arms around Chloe and squeezed tight. "You got this," she encouraged, searching her purse for keys.

"Yes! You got this," Jade repeated. "Call me if you need me. I won't be far." Jade hugged her sister again.

"Thanks for all your help, ladies." Chloe walked them to the door. The three embraced again. This time in a group hug.

Chloe pouted as they exited. Jade pouted, too. Jewel gave her an encouraging wink. Chloe nodded in response as an unspoken *I can do this.*

Watching as both sisters made their way down the walk and into their cars, Chloe began second-guessing herself. She wanted to back out. It was all too uncertain. How would El respond? Would she just get up and leave? What if she hit Joliet—or her for that matter? As refined as El was, Chloe truly didn't expect her to act violently but she knew El wouldn't take kindly to being blindsided.

Maybe they should have pushed this dinner off another week, but there was really no reason to prolong this any further. It was time for her to live openly. Donovan made her happier than any man she'd ever dated. She felt girly and giddy in his presence. The short amount of time when they weren't seeing each other regularly, she was miserable. Donovan proved himself to be more than a stand-up man. Chloe was glad he'd persisted. She could certainly see herself falling in love with him. Maybe she was already on her way there. The thought made Chloe smile.

Chloe heard her phone chirp. She headed back to the dining room to retrieve it. When she saw the time, she realized it was too late to call it off. El should be en route. The thought made Chloe's breath catch. Chloe hit the icon to see the message that had just come in and her bell rung. She froze.

Breathing in and out slowly, Chloe cautiously walked to the door. Seeing her mother's silhouette gave her pause. She forced herself the rest of the way to the door, speaking each action as she did it. "Open the door, Chloe." Mustering up any cheer she could find, Chloe swung the door open. "Mom!"

El's brows creased. "Yes, dear, it's me. You did invite me to dinner, right?"

Chloe laughed, stepping aside and admiring her mother's stylish, yellow silk shirt and pants of the same hue. "Come on in."

El shook her head at Chloe with a cautious grin and one raised brow. "I wonder about you sometimes."

"Nice purse," Chloe said, taking her mother's bag and setting it on the console in the entranceway.

"I got it during our last shopping spree. That was such fun."

"It was, wasn't it?" Chloe loved her mother's sweetheart-lipped smile but couldn't help but wonder how much longer that jovial look would last. "Come on in the kitchen. Would you like a glass of wine?"

"Sure. It smells wonderful in here." El halted and let out a slight gasp. "And you made my favorite—lemon pound cake." El closed her eyes and sniffed the air. "Hmm. I can't wait to get into it."

"Just for you." Chloe took two glasses from the counter and poured a glass of wine for both of them.

El sat on the bench in front of the island. "I was happy that you asked me to dinner." El took the glass from Chloe. "It's been so long since we spent time together. You know—just the two of us. I mean, we see each other every day at work but it's all about work and the past few weeks have been absolutely crazy." She sipped her wine. "Mm. Pretty good." She raised her glass. "I'm almost glad we didn't get that contract—well, maybe just a little—but now that the date has been changed to this coming Friday we would have been going nuts with it being so close to our reception." El rolled her eyes upward. "Could you imagine?"

"Nope. I don't want to imagine. I'm already swamped with the reception," Chloe said, leaning over the island counter with her glass in her hand. She was truly enjoying her mother's company and almost felt bad about what was about to happen. But it was necessary.

"By the way, did you ever find a dress? I'm going to use that one I got last week while we were out. I tried it on when I got home and it looked absolutely stunning and that's me being modest. Ha!" El slapped the countertop and laughed.

Chloe chuckled. "I'm sure I'll find something this week."

El slid off the stool and strutted toward the dining room with her perfect posture. "I want to see what you have in here that smells so amazing."

A nervous flutter squiggled through Chloe's stomach. She followed behind El.

"This looks fantastic. I taught you well." El walked around the table, taking in the setup. "This is a lot of food for two people."

"I'm expecting more people."

"Oh." El sounded slightly disappointed. "Are your sisters coming?"

"Actually—" The bell rang and Chloe couldn't find her voice to finish her sentence. She cleared her throat. "I'll get that."

Chloe sprinted to the door. Her hands trembled as she turned the knob. She paused to take a deep breath before pulling the door open. When she did, Joliet's pretty red-lipped smile immediately put her at ease. She smiled back, feeling thankful. Joliet's warm demeanor made her feel like things wouldn't be so bad.

"Thank you for coming, Mrs. Rivers." Chloe purposely didn't speak loudly. "Welcome." She stepped aside to let her and Donovan in.

Donovan kissed her cheek and she felt even more at ease when she saw Mrs. Rivers smile at his gesture.

"Who is it, honey?" El flowed from the dining room with her wine glass held high in the air and an inviting smile, all ready to greet their guest. El's eyes went to Joliet. She halted, frozen in place as if she'd hit a force field that wouldn't allow her to go any farther. A scowl replaced her smile. She reared back as if she smelled something putrid. "What? What is *she* doing here?" El spat out the word "she" as if it tasted bad in her mouth.

"Mom!" El shot daggers at Chloe with her eyes. Chloe felt them pierce her soul.

"Hello, El." Joliet's tone was stiff. She frowned.

El only blinked at Joliet. She didn't respond. The vein in her neck protruded and throbbed.

"Hello, Mrs. Chandler." Donovan pushed through the tense silence.

El walked toward the console, put her glass down and snatched her purse. "I don't know what kind of game you all are playing here but I want no part of it."

"Ma! Please."

"El doesn't need to go," Joliet said. "I'll leave."

"No!" Donovan's shout startled everyone. Three pairs of wide eyes landed on him at the same time. "We came here to accomplish something and with all due respect, no one is leaving until we do just that." Donovan stood by Chloe's side, placing his hand on the small of her back.

El glared at Donovan as if she were about to curse. She looked at Donovan's hand on Chloe and confusion covered her expression.

"Yes, Ma," Chloe said in a small voice. "We all need to talk."

"Chloe. What's this about?" El shifted her weight to one foot and folded her arms, exasperated. "And how long has this been going on?" She unfolded her arms and pointed back and forth between Chloe and Donovan.

"Let's all go into the dining room," Chloe said. Donovan took her hand and squeezed it gently. At that moment, Chloe was convinced that she was doing the right thing.

Joliet, Chloe and Donovan started toward the dining room. El didn't move. Chloe turned back and saw her mother stay stubbornly in place.

"Ma! Please. I need you to do this—for me."

El averted her eyes and huffed. After another beat, she marched past all of them. Chloe silently prayed for strength.

El sat down hard. "Someone start talking," El ordered.

Joliet looked at Chloe as if she pitied her. "El, it's obvious that our kids are in love," she said, smiling at her son with admiration.

Chloe was surprised that she didn't flinch at Joliet's choice of words. It seemed fitting. As extreme as this situation was, her words were appropriate. What else could draw this unlikely group together?

"It's obvious they're looking for our blessing."

"And they'll never get it," El spat.

"Mom!" Chloe chided.

"Don't 'Mom' me! How dare you do this to me?"

"Just listen, please!"

"We know that something happened between the two of you many years ago and we have reason to believe that it was all a huge misunderstanding."

"Humph!" El pursed her lips, stiffened her back and focused her attention on the wall.

"I'll start." Joliet sighed and then regarded Chloe with sympathetic eyes. "El." She turned to face El. "When my son came to me and told me he wanted to be with Chloe, I knew how hard this would be but he was adamant. I'm doing this for him—for them." Joliet took considerable pauses between each sentence. "Then he asked about us and all of the anger and pain came flooding back." Joliet's eyes glistened. She swallowed. "Then I realized I needed this as much as he did."

El turned slightly. Her posture softened when she realized Joliet was crying. Again, she looked confused.

"I never came on to Gary that night at his apartment." El faced her fully, narrowing her eyes. Joliet continued. "He forced himself on me. I had to…" Joliet swallowed. "I had to fight him. He ripped my clothes…" Joliet closed her eyes for a moment. "He pinned me against his couch and told me, 'You know you want me,'" Joliet mimicked his menacing voice. "Spit flew from his mouth as he spoke. I remember his breath smelling like liquor. I kicked…and kicked." Joliet panted, lost in her story as if she'd gone back in time. Tears rolled down Chloe's cheeks. El's face expressed bewilderment, her brows rose.

"He was so strong but I kept fighting. My knee landed in his groin. He let go of me and rolled onto the floor holding himself, screaming, calling me names—threatening to kill me. I ran and kept running until I made it all the way back to our dorm. You weren't there." Joliet pulled her lips in, pausing. "I took a shower, balled up the ripped-up clothes and put them in a bag in the bottom of my hamper. I tried to wait for you to come back to the dorm but you never came. I curled up in my bed and cried myself to sleep."

El's eyes were trained on Joliet. Her expression was stoic. Chloe tried but couldn't get a read on her. She wondered what was going through her mother's mind.

"I didn't go to my first class the next morning. You were still out. I assumed you stayed over at Gary's. When I finally did come out…" Joliet wiped the tears from her cheek. "Gary was waiting outside. He taunted me all the way to class, saying that he told you everything was my fault and that you believed him. I called him a liar." Joliet's voice was slightly hoarse now. "He threatened to hurt me if I told anyone—said he'd make me disappear. After class, he threatened me all the way back to our dorm." Joliet broke down, unable to speak anymore. Her shoulders rocked. Donovan ran to her side. His expression was dark. He held his mother.

Chloe went to El. Her eyes now glistened with tears, too.

Joliet got herself together. "He took everything from me. You, my freedom and no one would listen, not the school, our so-called friends, not even you." Joliet shook her head seeming to remember vividly. She squeezed her eyes shut. After a while, she looked up at El. "When you finally came back to the dorm, you were so angry. I couldn't believe you accepted his lies without question. There was no getting through to you. You were my friend," she said, shaking her head as if asking, *how could you?* Joliet sighed, then shrugged. "We were young." She pressed imaginary wrinkles from her skirt. "I changed dorms, started seeing a therapist, whom I never told the complete truth, because everyone else at school that I tried to tell only reminded me of what I was up against. One even mentioned that half the girls on campus was after Gary as if I should have been happy that he paid me any attention at all. Gary was the university's all-star. They doted on him. He said they'd never take my side against his and he was right. This kind of stuff happened, and still happens, on college campuses all the time. I never expected it to happen to me." Joliet straightened her back, tilted her head and looked over at El. "Eventually, I buried all of it—the memories, the pain— buried it so deep it was almost like it never happened. Hating you became normal."

El stood—eyes wide and spilling tears. She looked at no one and nothing in particular. Wiping away the tears, she cleared her throat and began to walk. Everyone watched. No one spoke. With one slow step at a time, El made her way over to Joliet.

"I had no idea," El said in a small voice when she finally reached Joliet. "Gary told me you were spreading lies about me around campus, telling our friends that I only wanted him because he was going pro. I believed him." El looked down at her fingers. "After the draft he just… stopped calling—ran off without looking back. I never heard from him again."

Joliet rose to meet her and for some time they just stood face-to-face. Tears continued falling from both pairs of eyes. Donovan and Chloe stood silently in the background, linked by a collective sense of hope.

Chapter 29

Donovan was exhausted. The week had been physically and emotionally taxing but he and Chloe had accomplished much. He finally took her out on the boat, recreating the night they sailed in Puerto Rico. They'd gotten their parents in the same room without fireworks twice. The two women even banded together to find Gary, who was serving time for sexually harassing one of his students. That news dispelled any possible doubts El had. A tearful apology set their relationship on a path of restoration.

Donovan and his parents attended Chloe's showcase for the restaurant the night before and he went home with her. The two were so tired all they could do was lie in one another's arms and sleep. Now his entire family was on deck to prepare for The Jacqueline Bosley Foundation's massive gala.

La Belle Riviere was a frenzy of noise and movement. Joliet gave orders along with all the other department heads. Every square inch of the place buzzed with activity. Normally Joliet wouldn't be involved on this level, but she also didn't normally have huge celebrities for clients who attracted hordes of local and national press.

Even with the last-minute change of date, Jacqueline managed to sell over four hundred tickets to the event at twenty-five hundred dollars each. That number didn't include the complimentary tickets for the press and cer-

212 *It Started in Paradise*

tain families on Long Island that Jacqueline personally invited—including the Chandlers and the owners of The Crest.

Donovan updated his spreadsheet to make a few more amendments to the expenses for this gala. Jacqueline had paid the balance the week before, but with all the recent changes and additional people, the foundation ended up with new charges. After printing the revised invoices, Donovan shut down his computer and headed home to get ready for the night's festivities.

Donovan walked into his house wishing he actually had time for a nap. He thought of Chloe and smiled. Seeing her in a beautiful ball gown would keep him invigorated. He hoped Jacqueline would be too preoccupied to be flirtatious. He didn't want Chloe getting any wrong ideas just when they were finally getting their relationship back on track. The idea of the two of them in the same room gave him temporary pause. He had nothing to hide but Jacqueline was insistent and she was an important client.

Donovan's turnaround was swift. Within forty-five minutes he was showered, in his tux and heading back to the catering hall. On the way, he'd checked in with Chloe to make sure she was still coming. By the time he returned, guests had begun to arrive. Flashes from the cameras of dozens of reporters captured attendees as they exited their cars. Donovan had personally never been but he imagined this was probably what the red carpets were like at those award shows on television.

Cocktail hour was in full swing. Donovan grew slightly anxious. He couldn't wait to see Chloe. He felt fortunate to actually have both their parents' blessings and hoped that his small maneuver for tonight would work out. That reminded him of something he needed to do. Donovan headed into the main room to speak with the band. His mother walked in just as he finished.

"You look great, Mom!" Donovan admired her ivory gown and pearl jewelry. "Are you ready for tonight?" he asked, leaning lower to kiss her cheek.

Joliet sighed. "I can't believe we pulled this off in such a short amount of time."

"You're great like that."

Joliet blushed, dipping her chin to her shoulder and then waved her hand dismissively at Donovan. "Oh, dear. Let's go be fabulous hosts." Joliet squared her shoulders, lifted her chin and sauntered toward the door.

Following his mother out, Donovan halted when he spotted Chloe, radiating as she glided through the entrance holding a small silver purse. Thoroughly, he regarded her, starting with the elegant sweep of hair across her forehead to her perfect bun and her beautiful flawless face, with proud upstanding cheekbones. The feminine curve of her neck swelled into sexy bare shoulders and gave him pause. Instinctively he bit his bottom lip, remembering the taste of her skin. The blue hue of Chloe's dress seemed electrifying. It held her shapely frame as if it understood how lucky it was to grace her curves. Silver shoes peeked from the hem of her dress as she walked. Chloe looked absolutely stunning—more than Donovan could have imagined. The male parts of him awakened.

Finally, Chloe noticed him watching. He tilted his head, smiled and walked straight to her. The only thing that he was aware of at that moment was Chloe. Her smiled beckoned him. He pulled her right into his arms and kissed her lips as if there was no one else in the room. He hoped he'd have enough control to pry himself away in an appropriate manner.

Donovan heard someone clear his or her throat. That pulled him out of his trance. Chloe blushed and put her hand to her lips to cover her tiny smile.

"Mr. and Mrs. Chandler." Donovan nodded, hugging

El before shaking Mr. Chandler's hand. He hadn't even noticed them.

"Donovan." Mr. Chandler held back his smile and glanced at El. She pursed her lips and shook her head. Donovan could see she held back a smile. "You seem to be pretty smitten with my daughter."

"Sir. With all due respect, I'm completely smitten by your daughter." Donovan looked at her adoringly. "She's an amazing woman."

"I won't argue with that." Bobby Dale chuckled deep. It was a mature laugh of distinguished men.

"All right, now," Jewel said. Everyone laughed. She swatted Donovan playfully before hugging him.

"Hey, Donovan." Jade was the next to receive Donovan's embrace.

"What's up, man?" Chris and Donovan shook hands.

"Enjoy the rest of the cocktail hour and I'll show you where you're sitting once we get inside." Donovan took Chloe's hand and led the family to an open table on the terrace.

"El, Bobby Dale, ladies, young man," Joliet greeted each of them one by one. She and El exchanged genuine smiles. "I'm glad you were able to make it. I'll have to give you the inside scoop on working with Jacqueline so that you can be prepared for next year."

"I'd appreciate that," El said.

"Has she arrived?"

"Not yet but I believe she'll be here shortly. The cocktail hour will be over in minutes."

El and Joliet talked for a few more moments when a gentleman in a tux began herding guests into the main hall. It took a while for all of them to file into the dining room and find their seats. The band played smooth jazz as peopled milled about, mingling and making introductions. Donovan led the Chandlers to their reserved table.

The music stopped and the guests quieted when the maître d' took the microphone to prepare the guests for Jacqueline's arrival. Everyone stood, the doors opened and the guests applauded as Jacqueline glided in with seven young teens around her all dressed as impeccably as her. Jacqueline walked to the center of the dance floor ushering the kids to join her. She then stepped back nearly blending into the attendees on the side and began clapping her hands. The applause grew louder as the teens bowed, gracefully managing being the center of attention.

Someone handed Jacqueline a microphone. "Let's give these amazing teens another round of applause!" The room erupted. Some whistled. "It is my pleasure to introduce to you our guests of honor for tonight." Jacqueline bowed respectfully toward them. They were led to a reserved table up front. "Thank you." Jacqueline took to the podium with a proud smile aimed at the young people.

The festivities started there. Jacqueline introduced her friend and fellow actor Brock Sanders who served as the emcee for the event. The room erupted into applause. Women swooned when he took to the stage. Brock announced the scholarship recipients, boasted of their great grades and community service and then let them speak about how the foundation helped to change their lives.

The evening seemed to soar by. Before Donovan knew it, the presentations were done, dinner was served, checks were written and people were having a good time on the dance floor, including Chloe and Donovan.

The setting was perfect. Donovan caught the band-leader's attention and gave him a discreet nod. He'd made sure to clear things with Jacqueline first. It would be a surprise to everyone else.

"Is everyone having a good time?" the bandleader asked.

"Yeah!" some yelled. A few hooted and one or two offered up a shrill whistle in response. Donovan was sure the champagne that had been flowing since the cocktail hour had something to do with the whistling and other unintelligible sounds.

"That's what I like to hear. Well, right now, we've got a treat for you. We've received a special request."

Jacqueline appeared onstage next to the bandleader. He handed her the microphone. "Ms. Chloe Chandler!" she yelled into the microphone, then pulled it away, mouthing *oops*. Throwing her head back, she laughed. "Can you please come to the stage?" Jacqueline's words slurred slightly.

Chloe's head reared back and her mouth fell open. She looked at Donovan. He shrugged and she narrowed her eyes at him suspiciously.

"You're being summoned, Ms. Chandler," he teased.

Chloe gathered the lower portion of her dress in her hands and made her way toward the stage. Donovan helped her up the few steps. Jade and Jewel appeared by Donovan's side.

"What are you up to, Donovan?" Jewel asked knowingly.

"Who, me?" He feigned innocence.

Both sisters looked at him suspiciously. Jewel twisted her lips.

"She's onstage. Is she going to sing?" Jade's enthusiasm was evident.

"Give it up for Ms. Chandler of the fabulous restaurant, Chandlers, on the marina. We all know who Chandler Food Corp is, I'm sure. I just love those sweet potato pies." Jacqueline giggled. "Would you do us the honor of gracing us with your amazing voice this evening?"

Chloe put her hand on her chest and looked down at Donovan. With a smile, she wagged her finger at him. "Sure." She nodded at Jacqueline.

"Wonderful! Before I give you this microphone, I have one thing to say." The room quieted. "That man over there..." Jacqueline looked over the crowd, squeezing her eyes tight in search of Donovan. "He's smitten by you and quite dedicated. He wouldn't give me the time of day and believe me, I tried getting it from him on a few occasions." Jacqueline winked and the crowd exploded with snickers and all-out laughter. "He's quite the catch, Chloe. You're a lucky lady."

Donovan's and Chloe's eyes met across the room again. For a moment they held each other in an indulgent gaze. Chloe smiled, shaking her head once again. Donovan felt his heart swell a little more.

"Ladies and gentlemen, without further ado, Ms. Chloe Chandler," Jacqueline announced. She handed Chloe the microphone, pulled her into a quick embrace and then sauntered off the stage tossing air kisses.

The band, already prepped, began playing the intro to Anita Baker's *You're My Angel*. Donovan looked over at El, whose hand had now covered her gaping mouth. She looked at her husband and Mr. Chandler opened his arms. El stepped in and melted against his chest.

Chloe closed her eyes, letting the music pour into her. Donovan had seen her do this so many times before. Chloe started humming the beginning notes. People coupled off on the dance floor. Some stood near the stage alongside Donovan, looking up at Chloe as if they were at a concert. Placing his hands in his tuxedo pants, Donovan enjoyed his perfect view of the woman he'd fallen so hard for.

As he anticipated, Chloe began singing and before long the crowd was mesmerized. It was as if she'd lifted them, transported them among the stars and then allowed them to all float back on her last few notes. She opened her eyes to a standing ovation.

Looking right at Donovan, she smiled. He kissed his

fingers and held them out to her. At the same time, they looked over at her parents. Even from a distance, he could tell that El had tears in her eyes. Mr. Chandler held her protectively, rubbing her back gingerly. Jacqueline ran on-stage and wrapped her arms around Chloe. When she let go, Chloe handed her the microphone.

"Wasn't that amazing? Oh! I never expected that. Chloe Chandler, you are incredible. It would be an honor if you would find time to work with some of our young people. We have singers that could certainly benefit from any insight you may have and your superb talent. Ladies and gentlemen, let's give Chloe another round of applause." The guests obliged.

Chloe gushed and Donovan made his way to the stage. Unable to contain his urges, he wrapped his arms around Chloe and pressed his lips against hers. He couldn't control himself around her lately. *Ooh*s and *ah*s rang out as the crowd cheered.

"Encore!" someone yelled.

"Yes!" Jacqueline agreed. "Sing something else for us."

"Okay." Chloe dropped Donovan's hand and took the microphone. Donovan loved that she was always willing to appease her audiences. Her confidence made her more beautiful. "What do you all want to hear?"

Suggestions popped out from the crowd. Chloe agreed to one of the upbeat recommendations. It was a good old party starter. She told the bandleader and they began playing. When the intro started, Chloe clapped her hands, prompting the audience to join her. She began belting out notes and within seconds, the dance floor was covered. Jacqueline, his parents, El and Mr. Chandler had gotten into the groove as well.

When Chloe finished that song, the crowd generously applauded again. She went to hand the microphone back to the bandleader and Donovan took it.

"Isn't she amazing?" he said, starting the crowd up again. Some yelled *yes*, others pumped fists in the air. "That's why I love her." Donovan realized what he said only after Chloe gasped—both hands covering her mouth. Chloe's hands moved from her mouth to her heart.

"You love me?" Chloe seemed dazed at first.

Lifting her chin, Donovan looked directly into her eyes. "I do."

Chloe leaped into his embrace. "Donovan, I love you, too!"

Squeezing Chloe in his arms, Donovan spun her around. He hadn't meant to make a public display of his affection but was glad his heart spoke on his behalf. Leading Chloe off the stage, they joined the others on the dance floor. Slowly, they swayed from side to side despite the upbeat tempo of the song that had been playing. As if following their lead, the music switched to a slow romantic melody as the lead singer serenaded them.

Chloe whispered the words of the song to Donovan as they danced. He closed his eyes and lost himself in the beauty of her voice. Leaning his forehead against hers, Donovan found her lips and kissed her between the words.

Donovan pulled back and looked her over—carefully considering each perfectly set facial feature. His study of her was deep and penetrating, ultimately settling on her brown eyes. "I want you to sing to me forever."

Chloe giggled. "I want to sing to you forever, Donovan Rivers," she said and then sang the next words in a perfect pitch. "For always." She lifted her chin for another kiss.

When their lips touched, Donovan felt as if they transcended time and space. Then he thought back to where it all started in Puerto Rico—in paradise.

* * * * *

Dear Reader,

I hope you truly enjoy taking this romantic and somewhat bumpy journey with Chloe Chandler and Donovan Rivers in my new series about the Chandler family. Could you ever imagine falling for the one person that your family could never accept? Chloe and Donovan seem to do just that. Donovan coaxes a side of Chloe to the surface that she had buried long ago. She starts to enjoy exploring her new self and sexy Donovan Rivers. Their affair begins as a fun little rendezvous in a lush, tropical setting in Puerto Rico, but desire follows them back to New York, where there's much at stake, like family loyalty and business contracts. Donovan doesn't only rock her world, he steals her heart, and now Chloe has to determine if she's going to please her family or please her heart and become Donovan's lady.

Enjoy the ride.

Ciao,

Nicki

Holding her hand, Donovan led the way to the balcony, welcoming the cooling ocean breeze. "Are you enjoying yourself?"

"Am I?" Chloe asked breathlessly, wiping her brow once again. "I haven't had this much fun in so long. Thanks."

Donovan's response was a smile. He looked out over the water, listening to the sound of the waves. Still holding her hand, they stood silently on the terrace, allowing the gentle wind to lick away the sweat generated from their sensual dance. Rays of moonlight bobbled on the water, inviting Donovan to the shore.

"Let's go," he whispered to Chloe, then he paid the bill and led her through the restaurant to the exit facing the sea. Donovan removed his shoes and rolled the hem of his pants to just above his ankles. Chloe followed suit, removing her sandals and knotting the end of her dress below her knees. Hand in hand, they walked to where the water met the sand. Chloe's hand felt good in his, as if it belonged. They stopped walking, still holding hands, and turned to watch the evening's light dance across the ripples in the midnight blue water.